ONGAR WRITING CIRCLE

sheila.melvin@

First publish

ISBN 9781731030627

Available at www.amazon.co.uk

Cover photo by Liz Barker
Text editing by Lin Hannam and Liz Barker
Book layout and logo design by Irene Malvezi
www.irenemalvezi.co.uk

ACKNOWLEDGEMENT

Our grateful thanks to Ed Harvey for all his work in submitting our book for online publication.

edharvey28@icloud.com

Enjoy the Read
Mike Palmer

Enjoy the book!
[illegible]

Best Wishes
Sheila

Happy Reading
Stephen Lawley.

ONGAR WRITING CIRCLE

In 2012 Anne Cassidy started a Writing Group at Ongar Library. This continued the rest of the year and proved to be very successful, but sadly with her many other commitments she was unable to continue.

In April 2013 I decided to approach The Library with a view to re-starting the Writing Group but as a Writing Circle. Not teacher led, but where each of us could bring our ideas and experiences, where we could learn from each other.

We held our first meeting at Ongar Library on 25th June 2013.

Since then we feel the group has gone from strength to strength. It changes, as all groups do. People's lives change. They move and are replaced by others with different experiences. This book is a prime example of that. This book has been designed, co-ordinated and produced by the group. Two people particularly need a mention, Liz Barker, Lin Hannam. They took leading roles and our grateful thanks go to them.

Sheila Melvin
Ongar Library Writing Circle 2019

CONTENTS

List of Photos and Figures:

FLASH FICTION... WHAT'S THAT?

It's an exercise we use in the group sometimes to sharpen our minds and concentrate our work.

Using no more than 300 words.

We choose three words at random, state a time limit (usually around 15 minutes) and write a story that is complete in itself.

We have included examples using two different selections of words, and are always surprised at the various ideas that emerge!

Have a read of our work and see what you think!

SMOOTH, LOVE AND WORSHIP

BOOKS, BOUNDARIES AND UMBRELLAS

PUELLA

Puella lived on the beach. After splitting with her boyfriend in Adelaide, she'd wandered steadily North & wound up in the Northern territories, alone. She'd somehow put together a ramshackle shack just above the highest waterline.

She loved it here. Everything talked to her. The rocks, the palm trees, the sun, but most of all, the sea itself. The rhythmic clashing of the toppling waves, the long shushing as the water drained back. Natural music.

She collected driftwood. Every day, weather permitting, she'd amble along to find the sea's creations; her long, matted, blonde hair sparkling in the sun. Each piece given to her spoke to her differently. Some quite rotted with barnacles & weed & a life's messy debris. Others caressed by its parent to a smooth finish. This was communication. This was art.

Her shack became a gallery for marine sculpture. Larger pieces became part of the fabric. Others formed an avenue leading to the makeshift door. Smaller works were taken inside. She communed.

Then, one ordinary day, she spotted what looked like a blob of oil, deepest black & shiny. Not oil, but solid, perfectly smooth & shaped like a large pear, or teardrop. She turned it over in her hand. Ebony, jet?

It polished up beautifully. And took pride of place in

her hut. She made a shrine for it.

She would stare into its darkness. There she found its name: Artemis, goddess of the wilderness.

Puella lived on instinct & feeling now. She knew what to do.

She stripped off all her clothes & threw them into the sea. She walked slowly home & prostrated herself before Artemis.

She couldn't remember all the words, but managed a firm, "I do."

Then whispered, staring into the essence of night, "With my body, I thee worship."

A short story containing the words
Smooth, Love And Worship.

SMOOTH, LOVE AND WORSHIP

"Well, I just worship the ground he walks on," declared Maise. Lydia looked up from her coffee at her friend and gave a gentle smile. They were enjoying their regular catch up in the village tearooms.

Maise, after five years as a widow had decided, initially with some trepidation, to start dating. Both women were in their early seventies and had met at the school gates when the children were young. Sharing yoga classes, computer classes, and of course the children's parties.

Maisie was slim, with short dyed hair, and full of energy. Lydia had piercing blue eyes, and long silver hair. Originally from Russia, but always mistaken for a Scandinavian.

Despite their long friendship, there was always a hint of mystery about Lydia. Occasionally Maisie had reflected on the fact that she knew little about her friend's early life. As nothing had ever been offered, she concluded that it was probably best not to ask.

As the waitress brought their cakes over, Maisie started to describe with joy and enthusiasm the latest trip she had been on with Alex. Like her, he was fairly new to the dating scene. His working life had been as an officer in the navy. After the untimely death of his only daughter, he and his wife had eventually decided to separate. It was amicable, but he soon realised the enormity of the step and knowing there was no going back, had thrown himself wholeheartedly into his career. A tall handsome man with a sharp brain, and a quick wit.

“We stayed in a fabulous hotel in Cornwall at the beautiful Lamorna Cove. Each day was just perfect. The sea was calm, the sand smooth as velvet, even dolphins were jumping. I can’t believe it – I’m in love!”

“Look Lydia, I hope you don’t mind darling, but I’ve asked him to come today, so that I can introduce you.”

The café door opened. Lydia looked up. The colour drained from her face.
Walking towards them was… Aleksey.

FINDING MYSELF

It was what seemed like a normal Sunday while I was worshipping at the local church, that I fell in love. It was not to the church, a spiritual group or a woman. This may seem strange, but for me it felt like smooth honey running over my body. I was in paradise. I had found myself. I am not sure how long I had been looking, it was many decades at least.

Going back to puberty, I felt like I never really fitted in while playing around the local housing estate or at school. I felt as if I was born into the wrong family.

At work it got worse. A 3-year apprenticeship, Technician, Engineer, then a Technical Manager - I hated it all. The job paid the bills and more. Yet I was too scared to follow my dreams. In fact, I was too scared to even have a dream. So I plodded on with promotion after promotion hoping it would get better.

I travelled the world on business and loved the kudos but not the role. The further I travelled from home, in business and 1st class, the more I was seen as an expert, a guru, the solver of everyone's business problems. I hid behind the global company. Eventually, three decades of this took its toll and I left after having spent time in "The Priory". It was the only way I could escape.

At last I was free. I set up my own company in training and coaching and moved on to helping the Long Term Unemployed for 5 years.

But it is only today, sitting here in church that I have found myself, the new me. What I have been looking for all my life. I am a writer.

SMOOTH LOVE WORSHIP

TURNING POINT

He sat quietly in the church, memories flooding back. In his childhood he and his parents had spent Sunday mornings here, and he recalled how he used to slide back and forth along the smooth wooden pews as a small boy. The feeling of being just slightly naughty returned to him, a wry smile on his face. As a child he'd thought of it as 'doing his bit to keep the seats clean', though his parents always told him to sit still and not fidget. The worship in those days was usually a selection from what he now thought of as old standard hymns, though as he mused over the books on the shelf he saw that they'd moved on to modern songs now.

How many years since he had been in this building? Too long, probably. He'd had a twenty-year police career, and lately caring for his wife through her cancer treatment had taken its toll on him.

Yet somehow he had held on to his faith in God.
Tomorrow he would again declare publicly his love for his wife, as he had on the occasion of their marriage all those years ago. Then her body would be consigned to the earth, what was that phrase he had thought of yesterday? Ah yes, "Then shall the body return to the earth that gave it."

And what would follow? The empty house filled with memories, the garden that had been her pride and joy, now both empty of any meaning for him. He couldn't stay there now.

Old urges returned, thoughts long buried surfaced in his mind.

Perhaps it was at last time to see if he could be the priest he'd always felt he should be.

A short story containing the words
Smooth, Love And Worship.

SMOOTH, LOVE AND WORSHIP

His Worship the Mayor loved his position of influence and power.

Over the years his smooth exterior, smart suits, convivial parties and a way of disarming with charm hid a Machiavellian mind, capable and determined to repel all opposition.

Many had tried, but none had succeeded and the despair of the opposition was that he would be there until he died. Teflon Theodore seemed to have no vices, no passions other than being Mayor, and no past. There was only one person who knew the secret to his demise, the one in whom the Mayor entrusted his deepest secrets.

Veronica Hamilton, his deputy Mayoress was cold and distant without a spark of passion, just the love of power. When they clashed in the council chamber there were no holds barred. There was no doubt they were not friends, perhaps even enemies.

As Theodore acknowledged the cheering crowd he stumbled but quickly recovered his composure and bent down to collect his papers lying on the floor. There was a whisper around the hall, as Theodore seemed to be taking a long time to reappear.

His trusted advisor, Doctor Sayed, moved along the line of dignitaries and bent down to help him. Too late, there was nothing he could do. The Mayor's one unsuspected enemy, his heart, had succeeded where his opponents had failed. It had stopped.

“Too much Veronica,” the doctor thought, chuckling to himself.

Yet another secret he would take to the grave.

SMOOTH, LOVE AND WORSHIP

He was a smooth operator alright. He loved to roam around the streets, adoring the females whenever he could. Everyone admired his sleek good looks, his brown eyes that gazed at you, taking you in with that sincere look in his eyes. Of course people knew what he was up to, it was pretty obvious.

The only time I have ever seen him angry was when a nun came towards him shaking her umbrella at him, for something she thought he had done. Fancy that? He went mad at her and gave as good as he got, but he was no match for the irate Catholic lady. Mind you it was funny because the nun was hitting him round the head, her fulsome garments blowing in the strong wind. We laughed because the nun knew what a rogue Perry was and seemed determined to give him a piece of her mind. Of course he was answering back, or tried to, but the nun was furious with him and she beat him around the head. I expect she knew that some poor female was pregnant by him - yet again.

But he was the kind of male that females worshipped despite his reputation. So handsome, he was one of those high bracket types that gets all the love from everyone he met.

One day, he went out the front door in his usual fashion to see what was occurring. Hair slicked back, holding himself tall and straight as he stepped out. He greeted people on the street, pleased to see the

gangs. Some of them patted him, and made a fuss of him, and he would wag his tail at them, always kind to others.
And he disappeared never to be seen again.........

BOOKS, BOUNDARIES AND UMBRELLAS

The umbrella bobbed along, a cheerful shocking pink against the grey buildings. She was barely visible through the driving rain. He kept watching it as he dodged through the traffic and ran to catch up.

Up the steps, through the revolving door. Pause to look around. More steps, double doors, peace. Dark wood panelling, deep shelves, imposing desk for the librarian. A few computers in the distance, people busy at the keyboards. There she was, looking at a map on screen. It showed the boundaries of the estate and the footpath that was going to disappear. He came closer and put his hand on her shoulder. Her yell shattered the peace of the library.

“What do you think you’re doing, frightening me like that?”

“I thought you might come here. It won’t do any good, you know.”

She sighed. “So I’m just supposed to give in easily, am I? We’ve used that path all our married lives. The children learnt to ride their bikes down it. It’s a shortcut to the shops. Without it, people will get in their cars - more traffic, more pollution. We have to stop it somehow.”

“They always win. They have the money. You might as well not bother.”

“Nothing would ever get done if everyone thought like that,”she said, moving to look at the legal books.

He scrolled through his phone while she searched the indexes.

“Look at this. I saw it down the footpath the other day. Unusual, isn’t it?”

She glanced at the image, then looked again.

“It looks just like that rare fritillary I saw in the paper the other day. They said it was nearly extinct. Josh, you’re brilliant! This could be just what we need!”

He smiled at her and picked up the umbrella.

BOOKS, BOUNDARIES AND UMBRELLAS

Joan was drenched by the time she ran through the door of the café, she had been caught in a downpour of rain, and had left her UMBRELLA back in the office.

Being on her lunch break, she had rushed to the library at the other end of the town, to return the three BOOKS she had out on loan.

Her boss was a stickler for time keeping. Now as she took refuge in the café from the weather, she knew she was pushing the BOUNDARIES, and would definitely be in trouble for being late back to the office.

As she sat at a table drinking a cup of coffee, the rain continued to pour outside. Through the steamed-up glass window, she caught sight of her boss running towards the door, arm in arm with Mrs Turner from the accounts department. They thought nobody knew of their friendly liaison, both were married. During office hours they behaved impeccably always keeping a fair distance apart.

Joan shrank back, grabbing a menu to hide her face in case they saw her and thought she was spying on them. They sat a short distance away with their backs to her totally wrapped up in each other.

Quietly Joan made a quick exit from the café, and ran all the way back to the office. Having dried her hair under the electric hand drier in the toilets, she reapplied her makeup, and was working hard by the time her boss walked into the office. He looked as if butter would not melt. None the wiser about her time keeping. Smiling smugly to herself she held a little secret that could be useful to mention on another occasion!

INTRODUCTION

SHEILA MELVIN

1. Wind From The Sea

2. Ghosts

3. The Storm

4. Ode To Love

5. Leaving Summer School

6. Autumn Leaves

7. Biography

WIND FROM THE SEA

He lay, his last resting place this he knew
Tracks from the door, were they coming or going
Into landscape barren and forbidding
The heavy sky, threatening, full of judgement.

Through ragged curtains, a non-existent breeze
Ragged for a life, for the things he had done
A face for the women he had left behind
Slits in a flapping blind reveal all he had neglected

Yet his mind refused to go to that last place
Until he saw again the flowers in the window
Dragged back to stand on the uneven paving
Waiting, waiting, for what was to come

Then and only then, the barren breeze
Swept inside and took his soul.

GHOSTS

Ghosts of a fortune lay in the old fish-boat
A boat so much part of my family's strife
A fortune that never materialised
But one that saved life upon life

Saving my Grandfather's brood from starvation
Giving the Women nets to mend
Giving the Children a school, lessons completed
Moving away, a different life to wend

We turning our talents away from the sea
Away from the smell and the harbour
Away from the neighbours, the friendship
Deserting the toil and the endless labour

From this distance we backward look
Projecting a romantic, childhood picture
Polishing the memories of long ago
Was it all just a great adventure?

Redundant now, no fish to catch
No purpose now that life long gone
Now held in the picture on the Art Gallery wall
Tears spring to my eyes, this is wrong, this is wrong.

Sheila Melvin

THE STORM

Moving slowly, the water gushing
Throwing itself against the car
Windows clouded with foam
Still we inch forward
Blind on all sides
Raging water all around

Bump, a little further
Blind into the abyss
Water pounding on the roof
Frightening me, threatening me
The only way is forward

Now I can hear the wind
Forceful. Unrelenting.
Rising over the horizon.
Anytime now it would hit us
Will we stand the force?

Beyond. I dare to hope
I think I see release
Release from this hell
We emerge into a watery sun
A sign says 'Drive off Safely'
'Please Return Soon'

ODE TO LOVE

Oh, how I loved to be in Love
When out of school
with the Head-boy who would give me a shove

He cared not of me
But I saw him as above
my reach, my Love, my Love

When I married, but not my Love
Not the head-boy who gave me that shove
I married a man, who later, I didn't love

I met again my very first Love
The one who gave me that shove
The boy from my school
Disappointment!
with age, he'd become quite a fool

LEAVING SUMMER SCHOOL

The Tree stood still
erect and proud
Each leaf a copy of the other
Some with the suggestion of
autumn at the edge

The Square lay quiet
damp, from last night's rain
Two people gently, thoughtfully, upon it
The cobbles shine pale, black moss
finds a home between them

We feel the sadness
the forlorn semi-emptiness
We are leaving, not now but soon
A car passes, slowly in the distance
soon soon, we will be gone

We leave the quietness behind
the stillness, the ourselves time
So short, so rare, so precious
Yet so full with friendly chatter
knowledge, caring and kindness

Leaving Summer School

Now we are gone, books
closed, good-buys said
Hustle, Bustle, to coach and car
Have we forgot, will we forget
or will our minds return to hold the moment

The calm tree, the quiet square
now belongs to others
Others sit in our place, others look
Claim the view, open books
claim the quiet square

AUTUMN LEAVES

"Morning Russel,"

"Oh Morning Gloria, sorry I'm a bit slow this morning, had a disturbed night." "Yes it was windy although it's quieter now. Thought I'd be blown over at one point."

"Do you see what I see?" Looking up immediately Glors spotted it.

She'd gone. During the night she must have just taken off. Not a goodbye, or safe journey, nothing.

Typical. Stuck-up, just because she had the top position. Not that I'm jealous of course you understand. She'd lived right at the top all summer, bit snooty. I remarked to Glors yesterday about her peculiar shade of red. Too much sunbathing when the sun was at its height if you ask me.

And Glors agreed straightaway. "You're right Russel, she said, she was a real show-off." But now if I look round, quite a few of our neighbours had left. Winter was defiantly coming.

"I say Glors you're beginning to look a bit different yourself. You got a new coat? I like that orangie colour."

Then I looked down and noticed my veins were beginning to show. Old age I guess.

The wind was picking-up again and many more of our summer friends were leaving. I began to feel a bit frightened and as I turned to look, Gloria left. Just floated down so elegantly, gracefully, it was touching. She joined the rest of our family under the old oak tree, ready to snuggle down for the winter.

I looked up and waited. I knew it was my turn soon and just prayed I would end-up near Gloria.

BIOGRAPHY

Sheila Melvin

I have been writing, off and on, as time allowed, for most of my adult life.

I've also been part of a number of different writing groups. During this time producing several booklets of my own writing, as well as contributing with others in group booklets. I write a mixture of Prose and Poetry.

Originally, I worked in Adult and Community Education. Later as a counsellor for Citizens Advice Bureau and Victim Support. Working mostly in East London Tower Blocks.

In recent years I co-ordinated ODBSS Ongar & District Bereavement Support Service.

sheila.melvin@gmail.com

INTRODUCTION

LIZ BARKER

ESSEX ROOTS

Brentwood. Burntwood. Clearing in the forest.
Ancient woodland hunted by Kings.
Roman soldiers marching through,
From Colchester down to London town,
Pilgrims too, along The Way to Canterbury and beyond,
Maybe to Santiago di Compostella, Cathederal
of St James.

Order in the country, governance and peace,
Orders of the Holy kind, religious men who preach.
Nuns inhabit cloisters, to pray and serve and teach.

1300's. Romans long gone. Richard II on the throne.
Poll tax levied, the people have had enough,
The government must go! John Ball priest and leader,
Passionate sermons enthral the peasants,
Who, working hard, are hardest hit.

Wat Tyler too speaks his truth and, led by these men,
The peasants revolt and march along
The Essex roads to London town,
Where workers of all kinds join but…
The fervour sadly short lived, has to die.
As Tyler and Ball are murdered,
The people crushed, can only cry. 1381.

Now, centuries later, their legacy only in a name.
The Wat Tyler Country Park.
Here, generations run and play
Oblivious to the blood and struggles,
Running, rooted, through this clay.

Time-line moving ever on,
The eighth Henry comes along,
King of power and of song,
Who seeks to disengage the State from Rome,
And thus the peoples' spiritual path
No longer allowed to be their own.

But voices speak still, as loudly can be heard,
Upon the crunching cobbled stones that make the road,
Herald soldiers' boots, the death squads come,
As priests with help can hide, if not too late,
Whilst others, unafraid, are taken to the martyrs' stake.

William Hunter was his name, man of Brentwood
Who came to suffer this dreadful fate.
And now a symbol to this day, amid the noise of traffic
As the shoppers, and cars go on their way,
A column stands that holds his name,
Familiar, yet sadly unobserved, remains.

Our soil, the earth alive today
Is nurtured by their blood;
The roots of our Soul fed
By the history, and herstory
Of all that has passed.

A time-line that will never end.

A STITCH IN TIME ...

Enrico Caruso played as she swayed
And placed the bottle down.
It was gin, then some rum,
Trying to delay the final placement
Of the veil.
The netting was full of tiny holes,
Her veil of tears, held in tightly
Yet wanting to flow. I cannot I know
But I don't want to go
Through with this.
Oh! Lord, if you exist
Show me how I might be free.
And yet, and yet...

He had been so hard to resist
At first,
But then he changed.
And once he had had his way
Wanted to be off to play
This game with others.

Too late now.
She had started to swell,
Eventually having to tell
In fear, the family.
Her father, back from the Great War,
Grabbed a gun, and as he left swore
Not to return until the promise
Had been secured, and would be made law.

Her mother came into the room now,
Bringing no joy or hope,
A face set to place the veil,
Walking to the chair where it lay
And picking it up… but a nail
Was in the way
Catching the net, and ripping a hole.
Too late! She screamed.
Silence.
They stared.

Mother rushed for the sewing box,
Needle and thread,
And she watched as the woman
Intently repaired,
What had now inescapably been ripped up in shreds.

Acutely aware of the last given chance,
She undid her dress, let it slip to the floor,
And hurriedly grabbed what she could from the door;
With her clothes and a bag, and a shawl for her head,
Her mother looked up, but nothing was said.
She urgently, silently, exited home,
Knowing in truth, she was now on her own.
But courage would force her to make a way through,
Now her and her child must find life anew.

JALALLABAD ROAD

Stepping, climbing, time defining
How far forward the line is drawn.
Cover over, dice is rolling
Work life balance, death defies
Comrades' safety notwithstanding.
Mortars firing. Shells are landing,
Hand held death with figures writhing,
Shadows leaving, shadows widening,
Re-evaluate, deciding
Worthwhile truths from army firing.

Generals follow, then take lead,
Every Afghan can succeed and
Embrace the power that men need.
Whilst women, who may hardly read,
Covered over, cannot breathe.
Prisoned home, with boundaries drawn,
The Tahliban would take it all.

A market place has shattered form
As bombs explode and death is born.
The vegetables are dressed in blood,
The fruit exploded body parts.
Security comes, but much too late,
A hopeless wish to seal the fate
Of humans who cannot debate
The lies, the truths, which implicate
Dogmatic fundamentalist mistakes.

Jalallabad Road

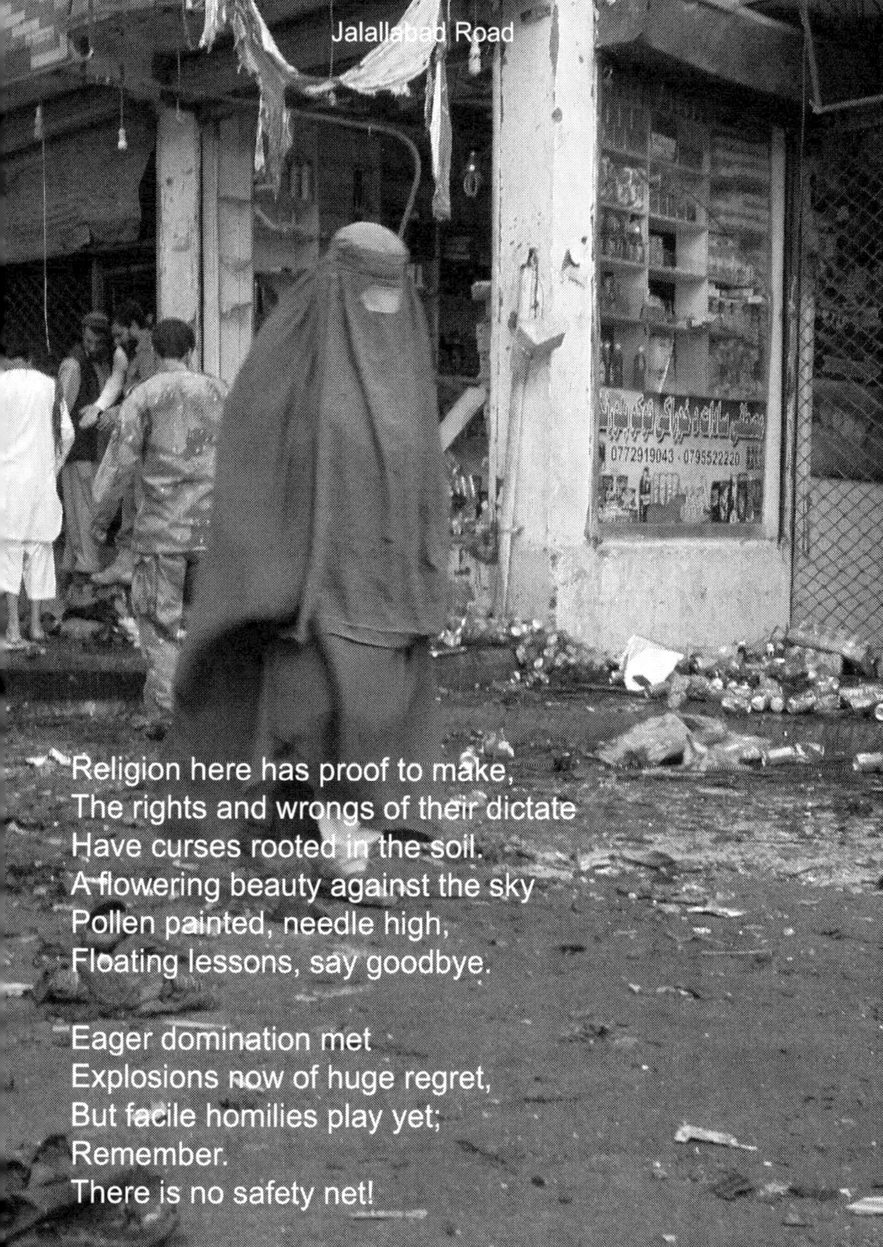

Religion here has proof to make,
The rights and wrongs of their dictate
Have curses rooted in the soil.
A flowering beauty against the sky
Pollen painted, needle high,
Floating lessons, say goodbye.

Eager domination met
Explosions now of huge regret,
But facile homilies play yet;
Remember.
There is no safety net!

DEVIN'S RAP

Devin, with a gift for comedy,
Sank his teeth into a doughnut
As a remedy.
Black skin, glasses, twenty four years alive,
Reachin' for a job inside
Waitin' to release his pride,
While his Mama was lookin' for a bride,
No love inside, inside, make me laugh
I need to hide,
I wanna step off this ride!

Hittin' a goal of my own,
Reachin' high, spreadin' wide,
Never let those preachers
Divide what ideas I have inside.
Spreadin' out wings to fly,
I don't need no church
To tell me how to get high.

Screamin', yelling', pulpit man,
Aint no friend of mine,
No matter how hard you might try
I understand your lie,
Seen you in the woods
With missy Irene,
Temptress Lady with a velvet skin
Dressin' up high,
With bracelets too,
Pantin' and a yellin' as she
Releases her comin' to you!

Service nearly ended,
My ears are a ringin',
The preacher's sweat is stingin'
And, as it drops to the floor,
The gates of hell are spinnin'
Waitin' for you to jump
Into those flames mister!

Mama starts to recite
The names in the Bible,
All those who are meant
To save my Soul, in revival.
She named me Devine
But I dropped the e,
I don't want no one to see me
As some preachers' son
Speakin' for the Lord in such intensity.

I'm gonna' live as a free man,
Buys a new wardrobe
To clothe myself in my own colours,
Leavin' the folds of their cloth,
Choosin' my own guides
And followin' after my own true love.

I think my Mary-Ann is the
One for me,
Sweet talkin', sweet kissin' beauty,
But above all, she's seein' crystal clearly,
That the most important need we both have,
Is to live this life, FREELY!

FREE TO LOVE

Love that doesn't trap or hold,
Or try to encase or mould,
That doesn't clip the wings that need to fly,
Or scream and yell when he or she
must say goodbye,
Where each one lives the life they choose,
Not fearing that they will always lose
When their love decides to leave their side,
And distance does not divide
The feelings that they have inside,
Exclusive rights are not enshrined
In attitudes of me and mine.

Where ownership is of the self,
And understanding can embrace the wealth
Of living life along the paths,
Directed purely by the Soul,
Experiencing love,
That makes one Whole.

WHAT I KNOW

The sun will rise and light our earth,
Its heat sustain us, allow us birth;
Our cells must move inhaling air,
As oxygen inflates our lungs
To breathe, allowing all repair.

Whilst nutrients exchange their gifts,
And molecules divide and shift,
Electrons splitting from their place
Create new orbits which have space.

Reacting swiftly to what comes,
Through eyes and minds and also mouths,
Keeping balance always hard,
The stuff comes in without a thought
For all the things these cells must sort!

The fats, the fruits, the veg and drink,
The milk, the cream, the lumps of meat,
The sugar, sweets and cans of drink
Swallowed whole, 'cos you don't think
About the acid you must create,
To break down all that's on your plate!

The rush is on to get it right;
The liver, kidneys are in fright,
Without their work you will be dead,
At times they throw it out instead!

Your stomach's full, the acid high,
And do you ever wonder why?
Diabetes on the brink
Can you swim or will you sink?

The tubes are clogged, the squeeze is on,
The heartbeat forced to push along
Your blood must flow,
But it's so hard this inner state,
When you can't see what you create,
How close you are,
To taking just one step too far!

So, look and smell, then make a choice,
And as you eat and drink, or smoke and laugh,
Remember then, that taking in is only part
Of what your body now must start.

Taste and chew and savour life,
But above all,
Please… learn to love your heart!

BIOGRAPHY

Liz Barker

Loves nature, walking, cycling, singing and dancing. Worked as an art model. Sold macrobiotic foods and books. Enjoyed amateur dramatics. Has a deep interest in spirituality and the healing arts. Was delighted to find the Ongar Writing Group in 2015 and is enormously grateful for the help it has given her in developing her writing, particularly in poetry, and also song writing.

She has a piece published in 'Essex Belongs to Us' available online and in Essex libraries.

lizbarker820@gmail.com

INTRODUCTION

STEPHEN LAWLEY

All my work is based on real life experiences.

1. The Identification
Is quite a harrowing piece.

2. My Lion King Moment With Adam
Is a touching life shifting moment with my son.

3. The Turkey & The City Boy
Is based on a true story telephone call before the financial crash of 2008.

4. Tools, Feelings & Africa
Is a short story about how your past can catch up with you in a flash.

5. WWKD? – A Man & His Socks
Is a humorous tale and has two titles combined, as the piece will clarify.

6. What Is The Worst Thing You Have Ever Done?
Is just a question, but it makes you think... Enjoy.

7. Parking With Mrs. P
Is a humorous, thought provoking drama involving my wife.

7. Biography

THE IDENTIFICATION

Kathryn was in shock and Andrew was in bed asleep, so I decided to go with the policemen to Harlow alone. I travelled in the back seat of the police car; I was feeling scared, dumb and frightened. The policemen were chatting both to each other and to me. The road was totally clear and it was the only time I wanted to meet traffic to slow us down. I could not remember another time when I had been in a police car even as a child. I remember the driver being inappropriate and trying to tell a silly story and the three of us all laughed. Why was I encouraging them to be silly? This was the most serious moment of my life. I decided to speak to God. "If this is not Adam, then I will never again question you exist. I will truly believe in the Almighty."

I checked again the policemen's uniforms for authenticity but unfortunately they seemed genuine. The policemen were young and inexperienced and were struggling to cope with the situation. Maybe they were just a little older than Andrew at 16, or Adam 21, or maybe they were 30? What difference did it make? We sat in silence for long stretches of the journey just looking out onto the empty A414 road. Please Adam don't be there. We travelled at breakneck speed. What is the rush? Dead is dead. I pinched myself, was this a nightmare? How was Kathryn coping, just waiting, with Andrew asleep? We skidded into the Princess Alexandra Hospital, and swung around to the rear entrance. I struggled out and inside, was left in a prison-like room. I paced up and down. If I couldn't identify the body, then some other poor parent would have to go through the same despair. I started to feel really sorry for them.

I was accompanied down lots of dark, eerie corridors. Through sets of double doors, and finally, to another seat facing thick, double doors. The policeman asked me, "Are you ready? You Ok?"

"Yes," I said grumpily. How the hell could I ever be ready for what was going to happen next?

I suddenly had this massive overwhelming feeling that Adam was not in the room in front of me. Adam always had such an exceptionally strong presence. I just knew Adam was not here, maybe not even anywhere in Essex.

The door opened I was beckoned in, and then asked to identify a young male, lying on a cooled slab. Immediately I was shocked. It was obviously Adam. I touched him and he was cold. I kissed him on the cheek. But already in some way though it was the body of Adam, it was not Adam. It was as if his personality had gone. "Get up Adam, we are going home!" As if I expected him to follow my order.

I now had to ring Kathryn, and report that her son was dead. I instinctively got out my 'phone and I went to press the redial button. Selfishly, it felt if I could just share the news, maybe it would take some of my pain away. I stopped. How could I pass on that news to a Mother waiting alone?

The policemen drove me back home. I was in a daze. They stopped at the triple gates. I staggered out of the car, punch drunk. Then I saw Kathryn running down the shingled drive in floods of tears. A Mother's instinct. She already knew. We hugged so tight, and then made some promises to each other.

Abridged from 'You Make Me Better - A Parent's Worst Nightmare'. Available on Amazon.co.uk

MY LION KING MOMENT WITH ADAM

We were on our empty French beach and I was jogging along. I prided myself on the length and speed of my morning runs. Then Adam came running from the side to join me. I slowed to let him catch up. We talked and jogged at a reasonable pace, father and son. He was nearly as tall as me now.

I noticed the pace increasing. My running partner had increased the pace and I instinctively increased mine to match his. A short way ahead, it happened again. I smiled across at Adam - we were now moving at a pace where we were not able to talk. Our bare foot strides were stretching out on the golden sand. It was fantastic.

Once more, the pace increased. I had to move into serious running mode. My heart started pumping hard and my legs were tingling. After a few minutes, Adam then said to me,"C'mon dad, let's go for it." I matched him stride for stride. Then, like a moment from Chariots of Fire, he started to pull ahead of me, even at this crazy pace. There was nothing in the world I could do, but watch the back of my son as he powered ahead of me. The boy had become a man.

Abridged from 'You Make Me Better - A Parent's Worst Nightmare'. Available on Amazon.co.uk

THE TURKEY & THE CITY BOY

"You will not believe it!" Erik was shrieking down the phone. It was the week before Christmas. It was unusual for him to be so expressive.
"Believe what?" I asked, genuinely excited for him.
"They have gone and done it!"
"Done what?"
"You just will not believe it," he repeated.
"Ok. I will if you tell me what it is, and who are they?"
"MG."

We had left school together, I went into the GPO/BT while he went to work for Row Rudd, as a city broker. Why I never joined him, I really do not know. I loved the idea of wearing a suit, and working in the city. It seemed like you were then important, compared to hairy arsed engineers, like me. Later, he moved on to MG - Morgan Grenville an international merchant, or was it an investment bank? I always remembered Erik in his cream coloured, tailored suits.

"What country are you in at the moment?" I enquired. I knew the answer, but wanted to give him some kudos.
"I'm in the city, and I have just had my review with the Director."

Erik was up and coming. They had flown him over to Saudi to install a new back office Stock Exchange system. His expertise was in the back office not on the trading floor. There was not a person who did not like Erik. He was always happy, hard–working, polite, non-offensive, and a brilliant communicator.

"So what happened?"
"Well, we discussed my two years in Saudi and he seemed pleased with all the progress." He stopped.
"And?" I could not wait to hear the news.
"Well, his final offer is £1/4 Million bonus and a turkey!"
"What!"
"Can you believe it?"

No, I could not. At the time, my salary was just over £100 a week and I thought I was doing really well. Bonuses were completely non-existent. If we could get a few hours off for Christmas shopping, that would be our bonus.

"He is trying to humiliate me?" Erik screeched.
"Look, don't worry about the turkey, just throw it away," I advised.
"Steve, it is not the turkey, that's fine. We all get one to take home, it's a city Christmas tradition".
"Well what is the problem?" I could not imagine. Clearly, I had a lot to learn.
"Steve, many of the traders are getting much more. What do you think I should do?"

Now I really could not take in this information coming down the phone. Had he gone mad, or was it a joke? Unlike our friend Rich, Erik was not known for practical jokes.
He then started reeling off the names of junior traders. Ordinary guys like us, nothing special, who were getting larger bonuses.

"Look Steve, what should I do?" he repeated.

It was rare that Erik asked for my view. I knew he was impressed with my oratory and negotiating skills, he later asked me to be best man at his wedding, but for everything else, he usually excelled. Take chess; he normally won three out of five games. But I think we both agreed I was better in the girl department. He once said that women prefer tall, dark haired, slim, hairy men like me. I never believed this was true, and now he was rich I certainly didn't believe it!

"Well Erik, let's have a think. What are your options?" My training was kicking in. I had to give us time to think. But what was there to think about? Surely, take the bonus and say thank you.
"I have already threatened to resign."
Oh no! I thought, the Saudi sun has finally got to him and he has gone mad.
"Other options?" I probed, needing more time.
"It is so humiliating… SO humiliating." He was stuck in this train of thought.
"I have just walked out, I thought I would ring you. You're good at negotiating."
Oh no! I was really feeling the pressure now to come up with a sensible way forward.
"Erik, go and get a large glass of water and drink it. Then take three, very deep, slow breaths. Do it NOW!" I insisted.
The line went dead. I waited and waited. It felt like an eternity.

At last he came back and spoke quietly,
“Well, he did say he would review the summer bonus favourably.”
“What? It is only for six months!”
“I guess thinking about it, I could accept the offer, and see if they deliver a bigger offer in the summer as he said they would.”
“Yes Erik. That sounds like a good idea.”
He ended the call, and went back in.

TOOLS, FEELINGS & AFRICA

It was early in the morning on the hottest Bank Holiday Monday on record. At the rear of my 'cave', I came across my ancient, bright yellow, metal toolbox. I recognized it immediately, remembering that at least a decade earlier I had lost the key. I was certain that when we moved house I would find the key, but I never did. In that moment, I decided not to open the box in my usual half-hearted way but it would be opened that morning. Definitely before Kathryn, my wife woke up. This would be me, against the box.

I found a heavy club hammer and a large screwdriver. I slid the screwdriver under the box lid touching the lock. With my first clout the box lid sprung open. I was a bit disappointed, as I had expected at least a two-hour battle!

Fears in my gut had already surfaced on seeing the bright yellow corporate colour. August 6th 1973 immediately sprung to mind. The day I joined the GPO General Post Office. I remembered receiving the box in 1976, as I neared the completion of my apprenticeship. I was working in a Strowger electro-mechanical telephone exchange environment, at the London Telecom Tower.

These tools had not been touched since 1979… nearly 40 years. The first interior tin boxes I saw were crippled with rust. I forced them open to find two usable Hilti nail-guns. As I went deeper into the main box I found two 12-volt soldering irons, a headlamp like a miner's lamp, spanners, bank cleaners, and tools for adjusting relays to 1,000th of a millimetre. Most of the tools amazingly, were still in good condition.

I felt a massive desire to be sick. It was like going into aversion therapy. After forty years, the feelings that were coming up were as strong as ever. The thought of fixing an intricate piece of electromechanical equipment with all its nuts, bolts, springs and cogs, was equivalent to someone, who was scared of heights being asked to climb Mount Everest. Or going to a funfair where everyone around you is having a great time while you are feeling sick inside.

For most of my engineering life I tried to hide my fears from the other engineers. They seemed to love messing around getting their hands dirty and would never ever have understood how I was feeling.

My survival strategy was to help them in a range of ways, with their college paper work, or matters outside work. They in turn were happy to oblige me with help when I struggled badly to fix equipment. Basically, anything I touched seemed to break, so I decided not to touch the intricate equipment. As I progressed I was responsible for my own equipment. Again, I found it all worked better if I never touched it! On one occasion, I had a piece of equipment that just kept going wrong.

I spent weeks worrying what to do about it, when another engineer noticed the fault. He took the whole selector apart, and rebuilt it completely in around thirty minutes. He was so proud of himself, but he will never know how pleased I was! I helped him with his college homework for months after that.

I could not stay in this environment, the pressure and anxiety was just too much. Thankfully when I got promoted, I moved on to the electro magnetic cores. These were the early stages of computerization and had no moving parts. My toolbox was left gathering dust. When I moved into management I took the box home. Slowly it got wedged into the back of the cellar. Eventually coming with us to the new house, like a dog that follows its owner around.

Looking at the toolbox now as I cleaned the rust off each item, I was sure that most people would just bin the lot. But no, there must be a use for these tools? I started to search high and low and investigate possibilities on Google. Eventually, successfully finding a UK Charity that sends specialized tools overseas. I arranged for them to collect the toolbox with all the tools later that week. It felt good knowing the tools would be going to a new home in Africa.

Adapted from 'You Make Me Better Too', my second book to be published on Amazon.co.uk in 2019.

WWKD? - A MAN & HIS SOCKS

While in Egypt I had been regularly waking at 5.30 for the jog to the pier followed by yoga and watching the sun as it rose over the Red Sea. But today, back in the UK I woke at 2.30 am. I tossed and turned quietly but could not get back to sleep. As I seemed to have lots of energy, I decided to do something useful. There were possibly a hundred things I could do, as we were only one year into the new house and most of that time we had been away. As I moved, I tripped over an extra large black bin liner sticking out from under the bed with another two overfilled plastic bags. My head hit the floor with a gentle thud, but it was enough for Kathryn to stir and ask,
"Stephen, what are you doing?"
"Nothing darling, go back to sleep," I lovingly suggested. I waited a few minutes and when I thought the coast was clear, I quietly removed the bags into the nearby on-suite.

Over the years I had hidden a bag, and thrown clean odd socks into it. Occasionally I would rummage through it to match up a few pairs, with the intension of sorting them all out. But never did.
'New house, New me,' I decided. I will conquer this task now. So after about an hour I had achieved about 20 or so pairs. I had focused on 'the low hanging fruit' as sales people say, i.e. the easy ones first, the white, the red, the multi-coloured pairs of socks. I was feeling quite satisfied. I had not reduced the pile by much. I carried on and on, each pairing was another triumph. Now each success was getting

further apart. I needed a system? What would other people do? It was an old management technique that I had used and taught to my younger staff. If you do not know what to do, think of the following:

1. What would your boss do?
2. What would your customers want you to do?
3. What would an expert in this field do?

I considered these options as I started to falter. I did not have a boss, a customer or know any experts in this field. I then remembered WWKD? What Would Kathy Do? My wife (boss/customer/expert), my guru. She would just quickly and purposefully attack the problem in a mindful and enjoyable way, probably listening to Radio 4,or some positive thinking guru on her i-Pad. I purposefully, happily, plodded on with this in mind, but I soon had a brain wave and went into computer machine mode. I started to put the massive pile into some order, with all the toes together, and all the colours from dark to light in order. I then attacked the next group of easy ones: the coloured toes on a dark sock, and the patterned and named socks: Ted Baker, the Nike tick, I even found one sock with Monday printed in orange on the foot. What happened to the rest of the week?

I had moved from the on-suite to the main bathroom, and had what seemed to be thousands of socks, lined up in various categories. Pop, long, sport, and even female socks. I started to bin all the old and holey ones, regardless of their partner. I then decided that it would be impossible to match some groups - they would just have to stay odd socks until I found more supplies.

I put away the odd grey, the brown, the multi coloured, the light ones until at last there was only one group left - black socks. I remembered Kathryn had regularly bought packs of 10 plain black socks, as I was forever mislaying socks. But my strategy seemed to have faltered. I was struggling. I still had 148 black socks left. 37 socks lined up in 4 rows on the bathroom floor. I found a few more pairs. I picked up one sock and like a computer checked it next to every sock until it matched. It was slow but seemed an infallible solution. I pushed ahead, sock by sock. My plastic bags were now brimming over with successfully paired socks.

It was like Stone Age man bringing his kill home. I was the victor. I just needed to continue, I must not fail at this simple task. It was a test of my manhood. It was soon after these thoughts that I heard a quiet voice from the bedroom.

"What are you doing Stephen, are you OK?"

"Fine darling," I lied.

My voice was tired and the floor was still covered in odd socks. The morning light was pouring in through the bathroom window.

I then heard Kathryn's footsteps coming along the hallway. I panicked, she must not see what I had been doing for the last five hours and I started stuffing socks into the black bin liner, but there was no time

left. I made a last minute dash and dived across the remaining socks to hide them from her.
As I looked up from my prey, I saw Kathryn peering around the door genuinely concerned. I had been caught like a naughty schoolboy reading a porn magazine on the toilet when his mother comes in.

“Oh no,” she retorted, “Do you want me to call the doctor, are you behaving strangely again?”
“No darling,” I said, “I am just having a little sort out.”

Abridged from ‘You Make Me Better Too’, my second book to be published on Amazon.co.uk in 2019.

WHAT IS THE WORST THING YOU HAVE EVER DONE?

What is the worst thing you have ever done? Well, what is it? Come-on spit it out? If you can't even talk it out, it really must be bad? It might be so awful that you can't even think about it, let alone talk about it? Well maybe I can't speak it out, but I might be able to write about mine.

It was before Andrew our second son and also before Adam. In my mind life is set either 'Before or After Adam.' It was definitely before Adam. Additionally, having completed 'You Make Me Better – A Parent's Worst Nightmare' - my first full-length published book, my peccadillo was not even mentioned in the book. Even reading between the lines no-one, not in the slightest way, would be able to work it out.

Are you thinking it must be a secret affair?
Is this because you have had one?
It is because of my strong conscience, that I would never marry unless I was going to stay faithful forever, from the day of my marriage onwards. It is one of the reasons I have never had, or will have, an affair. In a funny sort of way it has set me free from the temptations of the opposite sex. So no, it was not a clandestine affair.

It was before I got married. I was single, so how could it be so bad? Have I killed someone? This is not a throw away question. It is real and alive. I really do think I have the ability to kill. Maybe not like in the

movies with a gun shoot-out. That is too dramatic. But lets just imagine this scenario. A known convicted paedophile on the edge of a cliff and attempting to commit suicide because he is sure he will offend again, asks me for a little nudge to help him on his way. I think in the name of humanity, I am strong enough as a person to 'help' him, and live with the endless lifetime consequences of doubt.
But just think about some years later when it becomes widely known that he was not a paedophile and committed suicide because of the shame of being wrongly accused. How would I live with myself? This is hypothetical; I have not killed anyone, well not directly anyway. There are lots of ways to kill without pushing someone over a cliff or shooting them.

What about my mother–in-law? A not so old lady who was in some pain and 'someone' ups her morphine levels and she dies 'peacefully' in her sleep the next night. Is this not a form of euthanasia? Are we going down the euthanasia route behind the scenes? It may follow down a slippery path where does it end? This is one of the arguments against euthanasia. You can start with really genuine cases but they then lead on to more and more, where does it stop? Four percent of all deaths in the Netherlands are through euthanasia. A 17 year old has now been allowed to die this way in Belgium. But they shoot horses don't they? So why can we not have a sensible European policy that is open, honest and respectful? Will we keep on ignoring the difficult issues?

So, getting back to the worst thing I have ever done. What? You were expecting me just to come out with the worst thing I have ever done, Just like that… and in under 600 words!?

Abridged from 'You Make Me Better Too', my second book to be published on Amazon.co.uk in 2019.

PARKING WITH MRS. P

I have another confession. Kathryn, my wife, who I love to bits, is an exceptionally Positive Person; hence I sometimes called her Mrs P. I am sure you know the type. It is not if the glass is half full or half empty, it is always full and overflowing. There is abundance everywhere. An example is air. Humans do not breath in more air just in case there is not enough to go around. In normal circumstances, this is the same with water. We all just drink the amount we need, no more no less. Everything in life is like this with Kathryn.

When we've been shopping on a busy day the small local car park is normally always full. When Kathryn drives, or is a passenger in the car, then like a miracle, a place will surface at the last moment. Normally this place is very near to the supermarket entrance. This happens time and time again. Kathryn just smiles at me and points to the empty space if I have not seen it.

So why was I not totally happy when shopping with Kathryn, as we always found a car parking slot? In fact, I was willing there not to be an opening. So while Kathryn was being totally positive and seemed to know a space would manifest itself, I was using all the power I could muster to ensure that a space did not materialize.

On one occasion, when it looked like I had 'won' as there was not a space, I smugly stopped and was just about to claim victory, when instantly there was a knock on Kathryn's car window. The kind lady not only offered us her space, she also gave us the two remaining hours on her ticket. I just smiled angry as hell, and reversed into the empty space.

BIOGRAPHY

Stephen Lawley

Stephen Lawley joined the friendly Ongar Writing Circle two years ago with writer's block.
Since then he has been selected and published in 'Essex Belongs to Us', with the humorous story *'How My Wife became an Essex Girl'*. This inspired Stephen to finish his first full-length book, *'You Make Me Better - A Parent's Worst Nightmare'* published on Amazon.co.uk. An uplifting drama about his life before and after the accidental death of his 21-year-old son. The book sold two hundred copies in the first few months, with thirteen excellent reviews. This has inspired Stephen to work on a second book, *'You Make Me Better Too',* available in 2019. Both books have abridged short stories included here.

stephenklawley@gmail.com

INTRODUCTION

LINDA HANNAM

1. The Day Out
Tells a story about how life changes, and the freedom children had back in the fifties.

2. Once Upon A Time
Is about the aftermath of war.

3. The Driving Instructor
One of my many jobs in the past.

4. The Showrooms
A tale of bullying…

5. Goodbye
The sadness of war.

6. The Guardian Angel

7. Biography

THE DAY OUT

It was 1959, travelling on public transport was my method of getting about without the trepidation that children have today. Looking back I can see how different life was. We children were seen and not heard most of the time, but we were free to wander far and wide. Unless Dad picked me up in his Ford Anglia of course, which was a fancy car with a big, wide windscreen, a heater and a radio! Oh the luxury! It was a time for getting stuff and experiencing the new events that were happening.
I got the bus from Harlow, to Loughton. I remember it was green, and I sat up the top at the front all alone, fancy that!

My mate 'Little Lin' was waiting for me at Loughton bus garage. I wasn't exactly big myself, being quite small at under five foot in height, but she was even smaller, so it was 'Big Lin' and 'Little Lin' and we didn't even quibble at what would now be a derisory nickname for me. We all had names for each other. We had an 'Olive Oyl' (right spelling that even the teachers called her) and Betty Crocker, Ginger Marg, Gotcha Gocher, Hiya Cynth etc.
We bought our Red Rover tickets from the bus conductor, who duly rang them up for us. We then rushed up to the top deck, and of course sat at the very front. We were so excited, and as we travelled we waved to people in the streets. Naturally, they waved back at us, life was good.
We finally got to Earls Court Olympia exhibition centre, where they were holding 'The Boys and

Girls Exhibition'. In we went, and wandered around, with hundreds of other kids 'oohing and aaahing' at all the displays, and wondering why would we children need vegetable choppers, and rust proof knives? How to make vol au vents, simulated rides in helicopters, and information on how to join the army? We were fascinated by everything! The world of children versus the grown ups.
We watched the Fashion show, with the models all looking like Jean Shrimpton, very elegant and remote. One model kept waving to someone in the crowds as she bounced along the catwalk, and when we turned round there was no-one there! What was she seeing? The clothes were hilarious, so middle aged and foreign to us children, with little berets perched high on their heads, and fancy capes in tartan. The models were grown up women, and their looks didn't really mean much to us youngsters. Nothing like the young fashion that was steadily creeping in. I remember what we were wearing, mine was a simple shift dress in Black and Yellow stripes going horizontally across my flat chested body, and simple cream leather slip ons with a chisel toe. 'Little Lin' had her dropped waist dress, with pleats, in lavender cotton, and white sandals. Not frumpy at all, or grown up, just nice. So we were both in hysterics at the antics and looks of the models, prancing around with the heavily made up men in their sweaters and golfing trousers, golfing trousers?! Pointing at something in the distance and leaning on each other. Honestly what did they look

like?! A right load of posers! They would come out in tennis outfits, and riding kit, cracking their whips for goodness sake! We could only gaze in wonder at these creatures! Nothing to do with our lifestyles.

In the middle of the exhibition was the Arena, a dance floor, with rope and metal poles dividing the space around it. Lots of the kids were sitting on the solid barriers that were placed there as well. The disc jockey was playing records that were supposed to be in the 'Hit Parade'. Russ Conway a piano player, ('Sidesaddle' plonkety plonk!)Bobby Darin ('Mack the Knife!' Ghoulish) Frankie Vaughan ('Green Door!'), Lonnie Donegan, ('Battle of New Orleans') Elvis ('One Night With You!) and The Everly Brothers ('Dream Lover!') None of them appropriate for us kids were they? One record that will always stick in our minds, was The Brook Brothers singing 'We ainna gonna wash for a week!' It was about being kissed by a girl - and not wanting to wash her lipstick off - imagine! A catchy tune, played over and over and over again. I think the disc jockey liked it. Lin and I had a little dance around to it. There was one young man sitting on the side and he was miming drumming to this song. He was out of it, in the zone of the music, eyes closed, shaking his silly head. Lin and I nudged each other, and started watching him. Boys were targets of derision. We always took the rise out of people. No change there I'm afraid! No other tune will ever transfix us like that Brook Brothers one, as we stared at the young man, drumming with his imaginary sticks, even pressing his foot to imitate foot pedals. What a plonker! We laughed and laughed, he looked so stupid, and was so full of himself. He got all we could give, he must have known we were crying with laughter at him! All the time, he was nodding his head to the beat, eyes closed, so funny! Lin and I were helpless little girls. We couldn't breathe for hysterical laughter. We could always see the funny side of life, even as children. Humour is humour after all, and we always had it.

Finally we broke away, looked again at all the other exhibits, and decided we were going to go outside to the Earls Court Road. We found a restaurant, went in and ordered egg and chips, bread and butter and cups of tea for ourselves. Oh very grown up! The waitress didn't want to serve us until she really had to, but we didn't care, and sniggered to ourselves as she looked down her nose at us in a disdainful way. Thinking back we must have been a curiosity, two little blonde girls full of confidence.

Once we finished our lunch, we then went back into the Olympia Hall (you could in those days) and went to find the Arena to see what else was happening. There was a 'Twist Competition' going on, with young kids competing against each other until they were gradually eliminated. All sweating and intent on not being out! Lin and I twisted on the outside to the Chubby Checker 'Let's Twist Again!' record. The trick was to dance with a serious face, Lin and I were

trying not to smile, stern face Lin! The winner was announced, we all clapped him as he took his prize. He got a book and a medal! Then it was time to put on the other music...guess what it was? Yes! The Brook Brothers - 'I ainna gonna wash for a week!' Our Drummer Boy came back, held his imaginary sticks up and then began again. Lin and I collapsed into shaking heaps, we left to go home.
We were twelve years old, and even now when we meet we usually burst into song - guess what that is?!

Your sweet red lips just kissed my cheek, and I ainna gonna wash for a week! Oh no no! I ainna gonna wash for a week!

ONCE UPON A TIME

He came back to 'Blighty' in his demob suit, sitting on the train from Hull where he had disembarked from the troop ship. He had a large haversack with him, full of souvenirs from his time overseas. As he sat in the carriage, watching the world roll by, the East Anglian countryside turning into smoky London, he reflected that this was what he had been fighting for. His country! He had killed men and felt no remorse, it was dog eat dog over there after all. He looked forward to the heroes welcome back at Ma's house in Edmonton, what a knees up that will be! Seeing his young wife for the first time in a couple of years, his thoughts turned to sex with her!

After all the heavy duty celebrating, piano in the front room pounding out 'roll out the barrel!' etc. All the neighbours in, day and night partying! The brown ale flowed! Then it was reality...

The wife's Mother had remarried and was running a fish shop with her new husband, so the ground floor flat she rented was vacant. Me and the wife moved into the rat infested hole of a flat, and I hated it with every part of my being. Being the snob I was, I was used to living in a large semi-detached council house with a proper bathroom. My Mother ruled the house with a rod of iron with the old man an invalid, having been gassed in the war, sitting beside the fire all the time. All was spick and span discipline.

Not this slum of a place! What had I been missing?

DRIVING INSTRUCTOR

"Listen, just tell 'em that they are useless! Ask them where they had learnt to drive! Shake your head in despair, especially if it was with their husbands. Say you can't believe how many driving mistakes they have learned!
They will always turn the wheel crossing their arms, so that is a good one to point out!"
So began my job as a Driving Instructor. It was an ambition of mine, one to tick off my list of jobs to try. I applied and got the job; I was a young Mum of thirty two years old, very capable and confident that I could do a good job with Learner Drivers!

The owner of 'Sparrow Driving School' (yes I have changed the name) lived over at Waltham Abbey in ostentatious splendour. Over the top décor, more like an Arabian palace, full of gold furniture. I guessed that driving schools earned a lot of money for him. He had a fleet of learner cars with dual controls, and the logo was magnetically attached on each side of the vehicle, so you could take the logo off when you used it for your own personal use.
My Manager took me there, and I had to walk up and down in front of The Boss, turn and walk towards him, give a smile, shake his hand and say, "Hallo there my name is Lin, and I have come to teach you to drive properly." The boss then said to me, "Are you happily married Lin?". "Er yes," I replied. "Oh that's a pity, d'ya fool around?" I just smiled and said nothing - no I wasn't intimidated. Those days were like that! Yes really!

Once out on the road with my Learners, my work began to be quite interesting. Meeting the very nervous customers, putting their nerves to rest by talking to them calmly, I did a good job. My Manager had also said that if anyone asked if I was qualified as an Advanced Driving Instructor I had to say,
"Of course!"
That was alright until a policeman's wife asked me.
I had to fob her off with, "My exam is next week!"
Of course I passed! She forgot to ask anymore, so I was let off that problem.

My Learners were a mixed bunch but the heart breaking ones, were the recently widowed women who had never learnt to drive whilst their husbands were alive. The car would be sitting in their garage, just waiting for them to pass their test. I would get all their sadness and heartache, so it became a counselling job as well. As we drove along they would say, "Oh, my husband should see me now! He always said I was useless and would never learn to drive... especially when he was trying to teach me and lost his temper!" Yer right - note to self - never lose ones temper with them. I had dual controls so didn't feel over protective of the car, slam on the footbrake - danger ahead!

I had tough looking grown men, tattoos running up and down their arms, sweating and crying at Hockerill lights in Bishop's Stortford, "I can't do this Lin! I can't!" I would say - "Don't take any notice of all the bibbing behind us! Get the biting point, listen to the engine, that's it. Away we go! You can do this!" Oh, the look on their face when we smoothly drove off. I hope they are still driving around.

One of my learners was completely deaf. She could speak to me by lip reading, which was a bit difficult whilst learning to drive, so I devised the action of hitting the dashboard with a magazine if I wanted to give her instructions. That would be alright whilst we drove along in a straight line as we had an automatic gear change for her use. We coasted along through the lanes behind Harlow until we came to a left turn. I was banging on the dashboard for her to, "TURN LEFT CYNTHIA! TURN LEFT!" So she turned left, but silly me had not indicated that I wanted her to straighten up, and she drove us straight into the ditch. Ah, a bit of a problem....Cynthia was shaking and crying as we surveyed the upended car nose down in the ditch. Big head other drivers were hooting at us as they steered around the car. No help there! Fortunately one man stopped. We didn't have mobile 'phones in the '70s you see, so I was helpless. Between us we somehow managed to push the car back onto the straight muddy verge, put cardboard under the back wheels and reverse out of the predicament. My Learner was in despair, and before we got back in the car she said to me, "You do it, and I will pay you!" Erm ...that wasn't quite the idea!

One by one I got them through their driving tests, and me, young woman that I was, said to them in an important (pompous?) tone, “Now remember, just because you have passed your test, doesn’t mean you know it all, we are all learning and you have now got………… A LICENCE TO KILL!   Happy driving.”

THE SHOWROOMS

The young women and men who worked in the Electricity showrooms were all very lah -de -dah and did tend to look down their noses at their customers. I do believe they thought they were superior to others and could be quite intimidating to speak to. No-one liked going in there.

So when I saw the advertisement for part-time staff I didn't think I had much of a chance. But I did get the job, and because I could only work two days a week, Friday and Saturday, the showroom had to take on another part timer who did three days a week and all day Saturday. She too was a young mum, though she didn't seem to be very friendly. Always frowning and wouldn't speak to me if she could help it. I did try.

I soon learned what to do and loved speaking to the customers. In those days just by producing a rent book, even the women could sign up for hire purchase. Often I would say to the husband, "Why don't you go out and get a cup of tea while I sign up your wife for this new cooker?" One of my chief selling points was to get the husband on my side. Extolling the virtues of saving energy, and explaining that by quickly switching the hot plate off, it would still continue cooking. The male would think that was great. The wife would already know which cooker she wanted - usually 'The Tricity Marquis' (a great cooker), because she had been in before to check it out.

After a while the snooty members of staff started ganging up on me and the other part timer - saying very loudly, "Oh, the tone has gone down so low in this showroom. New staff are so common." When I went into the staff room, knowing I didn't like smoking, they would wait until I entered and then light up their cigarettes in unison. I was all keen to make friends, so didn't realise at first, until my natural exuberance took over and then I started to fight back. When they said about 'the Irish' and how they wouldn't touch Irish produce with a barge pole, I really didn't understand - I would tell them that Irish beef was cheaper. They would close their eyes and say how they boycotted 'Kerry Gold' butter as well, what on earth were they talking about?

One day I went into the staff room and found the other part-timer in floods of tears. Asking her what was wrong, she said, "Oh, I have got to leave this place, everyone has got it in for me. I need the money but I will have to tell my Husband that I cannot work here any longer!" I was puzzled as to why she felt that way and she said, "It's because I am Irish, they are always having a poke at me." Silly innocent me said, "Oh! I didn't know you were Irish. I thought you were Dutch or something." She started laughing. "Oh, you are priceless Lin. Bless you for making me laugh my dear girl." And from that day we were friends, and I realised why she was frightened to talk to anyone. There was such an anti-Irish atmosphere around. She was being bullied by the staff. They tried it with me but I didn't respond, and of course when customers asked especially for me, it made them dislike me even more. Result!

Another good way for them to dislike me was to post messages in the ladies lavatories - all very juvenile stuff I'm afraid, but they asked for it!
e.g. "This water has been passed by the management." Sixth form stuff.
My flirting with the market stall owners outside our showrooms didn't go down very well either. Especially when I had a customer in the showroom window demonstrating how a cooker worked. They would start cheering and clapping me after I had sold a product. Even the customers would take a bow.
I became top saleswoman, just working on the busiest days and being approachable and on the customers' side.

Gradually, little by little these female upstarts started talking to me. They had all been to further education, and thought they knew a lot. Summing me up as just a young mum was their mistake. But slowly they became my friends, we started laughing together (always a good ice breaker) and I was accepted as a valuable member of the showrooms. I think they were quite proud of my success in sales.

One day I signed up a man and his daughter for such a lot of electrical goods. They had proof of identity by showing me their rent card, and I duly took all the details down. They walked out with quite a lot of the items that they could carry, but the main bulk; a television, washing machine, cooker and a hoover were to be delivered. As it turned out they met the delivery man at the gate of the house they 'rented'. I sensed there was something shifty about this couple, and recognised the man from the past, he had worked as a security officer at an office I had worked in. I tried to think of his name, it wasn't the name on the rent card. But in all innocence I believed them both. Then I remembered his name, told the manager. Of course it was a scam, and they had made off with hundreds of pounds of stuff. I was the chief witness when the man and his daughter were eventually arrested for theft.

That ended those halcyon days of trusting people with just their rent cards as proof. The Showroom certainly lost its snobby label. We were lovely ladies enjoying our jobs, and serving our valued customers.

GOODBYE

I feasted my eyes on him, the smell of him, the height of him. I wanted to wrap myself around him to keep him safe.

I had to bend forward to hear his voice, he was so softly spoken, and I rested my hand on his arm in a moment of intimacy. I am always lost in admiration of him, he is so fine.

We had eye contact and laughed together as we sat and watched the play. It was a Terry Pratchett one called 'Mort'. We shared the author's nutty sense of humour - "You can escape everything except me!" Death (Mort) said in it.

He looks older than his years and I look younger, so an onlooker would have thought we were an 'item', or he was my 'Toy Boy!' Imagine? The joke is on them.

The end of the play came oh too soon, and we had our last lingering conversation underneath the frosty night of stars. I looked up at him and just at that moment a shooting star climbed the sky like a firework. It was so very cold and the sliver of moon that hung over us, looked like a film set.

I cannot bear to say goodbye, but must. I felt so very heavy hearted…

Helicopters whirring above, men shouting and chaos all around the camp are his world now.

The contrast at the army posting is stark. The noise, the dust, the injured lying on the ground, he finds he can hardly see straight as he runs for cover.

Feeling panicked and cold with fear in spite of the heat of the desert. His tears run down his sunburnt dusty cheeks causing rivulets on his hot face. His beautiful face is a mask of caked sand and mud.

His last words as the shell exploded behind him were… “MUM. OH MUM!”

A GUARDIAN ANGEL

I land at Stansted about 1 a.m. - I can hardly remember the flight, partly because I fly so often and because I am pre-occupied with thoughts about my sister Valerie. John had 'phoned me that Wednesday afternoon, sobbing to me that Valerie (and he) needed me.

I go to the hire car booth at the airport entrance, and a tired bored male staff member, asks the usual questions to increase my expenses of course.
"No, just the basics please - and whereabouts is the hire car?"
So off I go to look for the car. There is no sign for 'Cars R Us' anywhere in the vast car park. I am the only soul trudging along at that time in the morning, pulling my very noisy suitcase... A large bear of a man steps out of the shadows and walks towards me. I am that desperate that I have no fear and I say to him, "Excuse me, are you English? I cannot find the car I am supposed to be hiring!"
"No," he says, "I am Russian. I will help you."
He takes my suitcase and we then proceed to go up and down every darn aisle clicking my key to see if any car lights up!
We must have spent about twenty minutes just walking the length and breadth of all those cars! Over the road to the next car park, I see a car light flashing. It couldn't be any further from the airport, and my Russian escort is still with me. We finally get to my car. I am so relieved. I shake the enormous man's hand and thank him so much for his assistance.

"Have a good life!" I say.
"You too!" he replies and disappears. It is 1.45 a.m.
Security is strict at that time in the morning at the hospital, and twice the security guards ask my business.
Alone I enter the High Dependency Unit and find a distraught John. Then standing by Valerie as she fights for every breath.

I know she is dying - and a part of my heart is dying too.

BIOGRAPHY

Linda Hannam, here

I belong to Ongar Writing Circle, it has inspired and encouraged me to start writing.

I have had a large family of four sons, and many different exciting career moves.

Having travelled extensively and lived in Spain for quite a while, has given me lots of interesting experiences.

I have an opinion on everything and enjoy an enquiring mind, always learning new skills.

I sing, I dance I paint and now I write! I hope you enjoy my stories.

linhannam@yahoo.co.uk

INTRODUCTION

MICHAEL PALMER

1. Where There's Muck

2. The Sound Of Sirens

3. So Who's The Optimist Now?

4. Another World

5. A Hole In My Sock

6. A Stranger And A Friend

7. Biography

WHERE THERE'S MUCK

"There's another one Jim, more manure for the working class mushrooms."

"Yep, words of wisdom from above." said Bill.

A suited man with frayed trouser hems holding a piece of paper flapping in the wind, passed the two friends having a cigarette on the pallets. The man had an almost evangelical zeal to pin the missile on one of the many Fosdykes' factory notice boards. In a moment he pushed aside the heavy plastic curtain and disappeared into the labyrinth that made up the factory site.

A blast of cold air rounded the corner and a pile of pallets swayed uneasily. Jim flicked his cigarette stub to the ground. It sparked through the pallets' slats and hissed as a puddle of water extinguished its life.

"Worth a look Bill?"

"Waste of time Jim. The rumour mill broke the news long before it was posted on the notice board and if the rumours are right there's little we can do about it. The company is in its death-throws with redundancies and the plant closure just being confirmed."

"So you think it's true then?"

"Jim we know the problem and the solution. Our

products are being left behind. The R&D turkeys packed up being of any use years ago. Many of our apprentices have more management skill in their little finger than the entire board of golf swinging landed gentry."

"What will you do Bill?"

"Well for now enjoy the last gasp of my fag and at the end of the shift, share a pint with you before going home."

"Well I've saved a bit. There was never a fast enough horse to tempt me to try gambling my hard earned cash. The interest is not making me anything and I could do with a nest egg for the future."

"I'm banking on the lottery. My Missus has a feeling in her water we're coming into money. It's just been a long time coming."

"Bill you may not know it, but Mr Singh down at the newsagent loves your missus coming into his shop to buy her lottery tickets. It's keeping him in luxury!"

Bill half-laughed, half-grimaced, he knew it was too near the truth for comfort.

Both friends mused the same thoughts. They had been prudent, but what could you do against a tsunami when all you have is a bucket and spade with a sand castle as your only defence?"

"Come on Jim there's the whistle." They pushed through the plastic curtain into the noise, heat and melee of the factory workshop. On the stroke of five all the lathes, milling and grinding machines fell silent as if under the spell of an unseen conductor.

"Come on Bill lets go!"

They shut the metal lockers with a clang and wrapping their scarfs around their necks, buttoning up their donkey jackets and adjusting their caps, passed out into the dusk.

Gnats chased around the lenses of the neon street lights, spinning in a death dive earthwards. Swatting the largest of the insects out the way, they set off walking quickly down the road to the pub. The terraced houses with doors that opened straight onto the pavement, the allotments with rushes hissing in the wind and balls being kicked against the wall by the local lads, added a familiar but discomforting note of an uncertain future.

"I fancy the Miners Arms for a change. It's been renovated and it's got a cosy snug for a private conversation," said Jim.

"Good idea. You must have read my mind."

As they pushed open the snug door to their disappointment it was fully occupied with a group of suited serious-minded gents who immediately lowered their voices on seeing Jim and Bill.

"Come on into the lounge. There's sure to be a corner seat Bill."

"Ok, I'll grab the table. You get the beers in."

"Nice one! I'll remember that for next time."

The landlady beamed at the approaching Bill.
"Not seen you for a while."

"Mavis has put me on a short leash and I'm saving money for a new car."

"Never mind. What will you have?"

"Two pints of IPA. Straight glasses no handles Mavis."

"You guys never change. Go and sit with Jim and I'll bring them over."

The new red upholstered seats had a freshness to them.
"This is the life, Bill."

"Yes by gum the first sip always tastes the best. Here have a light."

"Thanks."
"Could do with more of this life style."

"Don't think we're going to get it unless a miracle happens."

"Give chance a chance."

In the silence both kept their very similar thoughts to themselves but into the silence, came the sound of conversation from the Snug next door. At the word Fosdykes, both friends sat upright and tuned into the conversation.

"It's a sitting target for a takeover. Move in quick, sort out the management, slim the product line, and reduce staff levels on the factory floor."

A glance between the two friends registered identical thoughts. They listened on.

"Look!! Our inside man, with frayed trousers and hand-me-down suit, has given us all we need to know. You can't better a 'passed-over manager' to give us the trump cards to play our hand. He's been well paid for the info."
"No one knows. No one suspects. Fosdykes would vanish overnight. It's been around for a 100 years but no one's going to miss them unless you're one of the employees."
The noise of shuffling chairs, a goodnight greeting

and the slam of the door signalled an empty snug.

Weeks later at Fosdykes, now under new management and a new name, there was an air of uncertainty. No one was quite sure how sudden wealth had come into Jim and Bill's lives. New cars, new houses and foreign holidays. All people knew was that they had come into a packet.

There were two unconnected celebrations at the Miners Arms a few days later.
In the snug, a quieter group were celebrating. The conversation was more discrete.

"How did anyone know about the takeover?" the broker quietly said to his partner.

"Whoever it was must have made a hell of a killing. We were lucky it was just the two investors. Any more concerns suggesting, 'insider dealing,' would have killed this sweet deal," replied his friend.

In the lounge Jim and Bill's leaving party was loud good natured and boisterous. Mavis pulled out all the stops. Live music, and mountains of food and drink flowing like water. It was an evening the Miners Arms would never forget. Slapping them, friends said,

"No wonder you were the first to accept a redundancy package after the takeover."
"Come on! How did you do it? You can tell us now!"

They all chorused.

“Well Jim, will it be me or you?” said Bill.

“Go on, Jim!”

“All I can say is that at Fosdykes we were like mushrooms kept in the dark and fed on manure. We just found some manure that turned straw into gold and not more than ten feet away!”

Laughter and shouts of, “Give us some of that manure then Jim!”

“Perhaps one day…”

THE SOUND OF THE SIRENS

The oxygen cylinders rattled in their cage as the wild eastern wind made them chatter. It was a bitterly cold winter's day. A hospital trolley pushed by two porters rattled by, on its way to a building on the other side of the car park.

My sister cuddled up against me. "Where are they taking that trolley?"

"No idea Rachel." But I had a good idea. "What a depressing place this hospital is Rachel."

What a difference a week makes. Mum looked so well then. The trip to the woods on one of those beautiful English winter days, with a hint of spring as the steam from the damp mossy floor of the wood, rose.

"Come on Rachel let's go and play hide and seek."

Racing around the glade it echoed to our playful cries until breathlessly, we leaned against a tree. Looking down at the scene below we watched as our parents surrounded by the rising mist, embraced each other. Standing transfixed and watching this very tender loving scene, it was us who were the intruders.

The atmosphere was broken as both parents looked around and surprised by the silence, called our names.
"Come on Rachel let's slip around the glade and

surprise them by coming up behind them."

"There you are. Where have you been?" Mum and Dad embraced us.

"Oh just having fun," anxious not to let them know that their shared moment of intimacy had been observed.

"Time to go." We piled into the back of the Austin 7 making our way home.

What a difference a day makes…flashing lights, ambulance men hurriedly climbing the stairs at our home. Mum strapped to a stretcher, lifted into the ambulance sped off with its bells and police escort. The Austin 7 reaching speeds never attained before followed behind and with squealing brakes, pulled up in the hospital car park, the overheated engine hissing.

Dad shouted, "Stay here until I get back OK?"

His command echoed in our ears as he disappeared through a door into one of the many hospital corridors. As the hours passed and the temperature in the car dropped from hot to chilly to cold we ventured out into the car park, our coats wrapped around us to keep out the cold.

With the need for warmth overcoming our anxiety

at disobeying Dad's instructions, we crossed the car park and heard the chiming rattling oxygen bottles, sounding a note of doom.

Our thoughts mingled with each other. Doubt, fear and worry pressing in, matching the chilly winter weather.

What if Mum died?

What if Dad remarried?

What if we were farmed out because Dad couldn't cope?

These unspoken thoughts telepathically shared between us. The late evening dusk turned to night, dark as our thoughts. As dark as our future.

The lawn was enclosed by a quad of two storey buildings lit by a crazy swinging lantern that shouted a warning,like a siren warning ships of rocks ahead. Could Mum have been on that trolley going to that isolated cheerless building? What was happening?

I held my sister's hand as I kicked the kerbstone surrounding the lawn. Suddenly a light shone from a downstairs window and a hand beckoned us. We both froze. It was Dad waving us over. Apprehensively we made our way over to the glistening frosted grass, leaving a trail of footprints we approached a window. Inside the room was a bed.

Mum, half-awake, half-asleep, smiled at us. Exhausted, her eyes closed.

In a whisper, Dad said, “It’s going to be OK, but it will take a while before Mum is home. Go back to the car and I’ll join you soon.”

So many times we’d hear that phrase. So many times we’d hear the oxygen cylinder’s rattle and visit that open window across the lawn.

SO WHO'S THE OPTIMIST NOW?

The optimist assumes the road is clear, the motorway free of traffic for the entire journey. There is time to slow down on the way as the route passes through the South Downs with its wood covered slopes. The optimist leaves at the exact time it takes from Brentwood to Portsmouth harbour.

The pessimist knows the road will be filled with like minded optimists taking advantage of a beautiful Bank Holiday weekend. The pessimist is the person who insists on getting to the coach station an hour early to catch the midday coach arriving just in time to see the tail lights of the delayed 10.00 coach leaving the bus station. Time then for the tasteless tea or watery coffee with stale Eccles cake and a curly edged sandwich!

Both were right, a rarity in life. The optimist flew over the QE II Bridge crossing the Thames at a speed that barely left him time to catch the vista of the river 200 feet below, or the Eurostar, speeding silvery snake entering the tunnel under the Thames onward to Paris. The pessimist looked at the stationary traffic waiting to enter the tunnel joining Kent to Essex. Traffic lined up not feet or even yards but mile after mile. The vibes of anxious occupants wondering if they would get to Stansted in time for their flight and those who already knew they would not.

The pessimist turning to the optimist said, “If you were in that traffic jam you would be a Damascus convert to the pessimist cause!”

The lorry driver had a fraught crossing from Dover and with heavy traffic was making a slow journey up the M20 onto the M26 and thereafter the M25. His Polish nature made him watch the miles from Krakow to Reading patiently pass as a matter of course, inevitable as night followed day. He couldn't count the number of times he had made this journey. His usual stop was Clackett Lane but being behind schedule he passed the service station with regret. Fuel OK, engine temperature fine, just the wind whipping round his lorry causing a slight sway but all was well.

A motorist flashed and waved and, as he passed the Leatherhead junction, so did another one. What a friendly lot. Perhaps the English reserve was changing.

It was only as he passed the A3 junction with motorists now hooting and flashing, that he looked closely in the mirror. Smoke was coming from the rear of his lorry. Blown away by the air stream passing over the front of the cab, he hadn't noticed it until now.

The blue lights and sirens flagged him down. When he pulled over onto the hard shoulder the policeman shouted, "Switch off and get out!" His English although limited, needed no second bidding. Gathering up what few personal belongings he had, he jumped down and ran towards the police cars. The whoosh of the flames followed by a cloud of smoke, left him coughing and with a few singed hairs. "Get down behind us… you OK?... You were lucky!"

"Some luck," thought the Polish driver.

More blue lights more sirens as foam was pumped over the blazing truck.

"Here you are mate. Have a cup of tea."

"Ah, the English answer to everything," said the driver.

"Not quite mate, that's why we use the fire brigade as well."

About 10 miles behind the Polish driver the optimist assured the pessimist all was well as they sped towards the A3.

"So I'm right?" said the optimist.

"And so am I," said the pessimist.

The traffic slowed then stopped with smoke rising in the distance. The sirens of the fire fighter racing from behind along the hard shoulder, firstly one then another, followed closely by an Ambulance. The urgent tone of their sirens decreasing in volume, as they travelled further past. We may be here for a while both the optimist and the pessimist thought in silence.

“Told you we would miss the ferry,” said the pessimist as the Sat Nav confirmed the impossibility of reaching the port before the ferry to the Isle of Wight departed.

“You’re right,” said the optimist, “but now we’re moving and about to join the A3, which looks pretty clear, we can slow down and take in the surrounding countryside and catch the next ferry.”

“You mean miss that one as well?” said the pessimist.

“You will never change! said the optimist... I’m just glad I’m not married to you.”

ANOTHER WORLD

The railway line passes under Copnor Bridge from London Waterloo to Portsmouth Harbour, a humped back bridge cursed by lorry drivers, loved by lovers and missed by every German bomber in the war. The bridge was a great divide, two communities separated by a common language. Both always thought their side was the best place to be.

The road slips down to the left with the Copnor bowling green and then sharp right. The Russian Orthodox Church with its imposing facade and rich icons inside blessed by the priest, in sharp contrast to the Tangiers Baptist church 200 yards on the left. Its brick front and stepped outer sides show non-conformity at its most strident. Tangiers road with the post office, Co-op, cafe, shops and churches bustled and was doing its best to put the war behind it. There was austerity but there were areas that had been hit harder and with greater damage. Mend and make do, second hand clothes and hand me downs were part of life. The euphoria at the end of the war was replaced with the reality that the peace was going to take a lot longer.

There were few new things, so the appearance of something as shiny as a Silver Cross pram with its ivory coloured handle and gleaming chrome wheels brought admiring glances and envious thoughts.
The Rolls Royce of prams! Shell shaped body, independent suspension and wide canvas hood, securely fastened with round serrated chrome wheels.

Phyllis sat down in the cafe, with its open front courtesy of the German bombs, drinking her cup of tea. A cry from the pram made her rock the handle in an attempt to quieten the baby, hoping to finish her cup of tea in peace. No such chance and with a sigh, putting her cup on the table, she lifted the baby boy onto her lap.

"What a bonnie boy."

Looking up Phyllis saw an old lady smiling down at the baby. Her clothes were badly worn, a scarf around her neck and missing teeth, which made her smile seem sinister rather than inviting.

"May I hold him?"

A little alarmed but only hesitating slightly, Phyllis gently placed her son into the arms of the lady.
On looking more closely Phyllis thought she had a gipsy look about her and the smell of smoke and yellowed fingers made her a heavy smoker...so what? The war had changed people's habits. What might have been frowned upon in 1940 hardly raised an eyebrow in 1945.
There was an atmosphere of living for today being of great importance as for so many, tomorrow never came.

Phyllis recalled a night of heavy bombing on the 24 May 1941. She could have died ten times over but in total oblivion, she walked down the centre of the road through Landport, as the houses blazing from floor to floor, were being doused with water to try and stop the fire spreading.

Phyllis was a signaller WREN at the Naval HQ in Portsmouth dockyard. The signal she had received from the Fleet about the tragic loss of HMS Hood weighed heavily on her mind. So many lost, some of whom had been her friends.

The shouts of the Air Raid Warden to come into the shelter or be killed were just an echo in her mind. She walked on ignoring them under a rainbow arch of fire and water. A flash of light, searing heat and a terrifying noise threw her to the ground.

"You had better come with me." Phyllis felt the strong arms of a man take her into a dark room, smelling of fear and sweat. Concerned voices murmured.

"Is she alright?"

"You must have a guardian angel. There have been so many casualties and there you were, walking oblivious to all the incendiaries and landmines coming through unscathed, apart from that nasty bump on your head."

Next day she walked back the same way to her post underneath the bomb proof Naval base in the dockyard. When passing the Air Raid Shelter that she had declined to enter the previous evening, they were collecting all the bodies following a direct hit on it. No survivors.

It hit hard. She screamed and shook with fear at the thought of being one of those bodies. Last night in real danger she had felt nothing. It was now, in the smoky silence of safety, that fear surrounded her.

Why should she worry about an old lady cooing over her baby?

“What’s his name?”

“Michael.”

Michael gripped the finger of the old lady.

“He has a strong grip.”

Phyllis smiled. Of all the comments she could have made this seemed the strangest one.

“Yes, and good lungs!”

The gipsy looked into Phyllis’ eyes and for the first time she saw a warmth and understanding, the awareness of a wisdom and knowledge of life.

“Let me look at his hand” she said, and she peeled

open Michael's tightly gripped fist.

The silence between them took them out of the present and into another world. This world had no need of the material things of life with all their distortions of human values, more an aura of a spiritual world... a world where the values of love, peace and total understanding of all the questions of life seemed to be revealed. At the same time there was no need to know fear, uncertainty or doubt.

"Michael will have a long life... he will have the choice to choose good things or ignore them... he will be blessed with an inner strength to help him over the bad times."
Phyllis had never experienced this before and felt a mixture of happiness, suspicion and fear.

"So all's well that ends well," Phyllis muttered.
"We have the choice to either make it happen, or not."

The loud bump of another pram hitting the table brought her back to the reality of the present day.

"Hi Phyllis, Hi Yolanda. You two know each other?"

"Oh yes. Yolanda has a large plot on the allotments and a shack where she lives. Mine is the next plot."

Yolanda looked up and greeted Iris.
Benjamin awoke with a jolt and showed his

disapproval with a sudden shout.

“Ah never mind Benjamin, he has a very loud voice.”

Bert the cafe proprietor came out and busied himself at the next table but he fell, knocking over the table and sending the cups and glasses crashing to the floor.

“Who left their blasted handbag on the floor?” he moaned, picking himself and the table up.

What he really meant was, that blasted Yolanda was making a nuisance of herself.
He never liked her and felt annoyed that falling over had played into her hands and made him look a fool.

“You go inside Bert and see to a customer.”

His wife was a tough businesswoman who had come from the school of hard knocks. The cafe had just survived the war. Business was touch and go and the last thing she needed was Bert upsetting the customers.

“Ah, two lovely babies,” she cooed, ingratiating herself with the ladies.

“Sorry, soon have this cleaned up.”
That’s a couple of glasses and a cup that would cost to replace. Bert was becoming more clumsy by the day she thought.

Yolanda stood up, gathered her assortment of clothes and said goodbye.

“Good to meet you Phyllis and Michael. Come round and see me sometime.”

Phyllis looked at her, the strangest of invitations, but one she would accept...although perhaps not mention it to Arthur her husband at this stage, and certainly not tell him what Yolanda had said.

Gathering up Michael in her arms and gently laying him in the pram, she heard the sound of a metal object. A silver sixpence had fallen from Michael’s unclasped fist. It glinted as she picked it up, brand new, a charmed gift from the gypsy.

A HOLE IN MY SOCK

"You know how to avoid the problem of one good sock one bad sock?"

"No."

"Darn it. You get a mushroom, darning needle and some wool."

"Sounds exciting. Problem is I don't have any of those items... and if I did, I wouldn't know what to do or have the patience to do it."

"Well do it while you are watching that rubbish football team you support. It might make you better tempered when they lose, which is virtually every week!"

"Grieving is a solitary time and sharing it with a mushroom seems irreligious to the boys in blue… and it's not a very masculine practice."

"Why don't you watch Sewing Bee and that posh Saville Row tailor then?"

"That's entertainment and informative," he replied. "I would rather let my big toe wiggle around inside my shoe."

"You need to get lucky. Try for a hole in one, you have plenty of practise at home."

"No… that's too expensive. I could buy a shop full of

socks with the cost of drinks for everyone."

"Has anyone ever called you mean? 'cause if there was a silver cup for meanness, you would win it!"

"Not a chance with you then?"

"Well, I am thinking of reducing outgoings by being more careful with my socks."

"You mean like cutting your toe nails to stop the sock being guillotined every time you put them on?
I throw so many of your single socks away."

"What!! I wondered why my sock draw was nearly empty."

"Never mind, you're going to get a nice Christmas present... you'll never have to worry about your socks again."

"Fifty pairs all the same and a mushroom."

"Ah, now I know why I love you."

A STRANGER AND A FRIEND

Did I know Hedley?

Yes and no.

He was a friend but it was not the average friendship.

No one knew what Hedley did...whatever it was kept him in a very comfortable lifestyle, which involved travelling. He would suddenly disappear and then unexpectedly resurface.

He loved the company of ladies and they reciprocated no doubt drawn by his charm, humour and physique. He also enjoyed men's company, was competitive and good at golf and sailing. A rare breed, being able to communicate so effectively with both sexes.

His mother was a refined, educated and charming lady, whose great pleasure in life was working in the old walled garden of her beautiful West Sussex cottage. He never knew his father, who had disappeared before his entry into the world. She was the only person who fully understood him and the love between them was palpable. I often wondered if she was the only real love of his life.

Hedley had disappeared for months and people stopped asking after him. Not sure why I was considered to be the source of knowledge on the whereabouts of Hedley.

That Friday morning the telephone rang in the hall.

"Don't worry I'll get it Darling."

"Hello?"

"Its me. You may need to do me a favour."

"Who is it Stuart?"

"No one Darling."

"If that's Hedley, tell him I'll chop his balls off if he comes anywhere near here."

Funny, I thought Hedley was so good with women but there had to be exceptions to every rule and Maggie was top of the list.

"Got a pen... take this number down and call it if I haven't contacted you in the next 24 hours." The line went dead.

So what was Hedley doing in La Langes? The road north from Biarritz slipped through the narrow valleys, passing the last of the communities of the fashionable town. Gripping the steering wheel and at the same time moving forward on the seat to get some air on the back of his sweat soaked shirt, he relaxed and settled into the long journey to Bordeaux.

He looked at the lorry in front of him, a large container full of fruit probably going to the Paris market and wondered what kind of qualities were needed to be a long distance lorry driver. Hedley felt he was following an old friend. The friendship only lasted another ten minutes. The red lights of the lorries slowing down and exiting left could only mean one thing. There was a toll road ahead and all the lorries were exiting onto a secondary road to avoid payment.

Damn it, these tolls were getting expensive. He flicked the indicator switch and joined the slow line of traffic heading for the slip road.

The long queue filled the air with diesel fumes. The road junction gave a choice. Left or right. Grasping for the map, it slid down the side of the seat. Ouch! The two signs left and right showed the names of Hossego and St Jean de Marsacq. Pretty places, but which one? In an instinctive move, which assumed the guy in front must know where he was going, Hedley turned left behind the lorry.

A sense of loneliness overcame him. He was lost in the middle of nowhere. The Lands department in Aquitaine had the right soil for growing trees and not much else. The forest thickened, darkening the sky and producing a low mist along the road. Hedley thought he'd just explore, not being in that much of a hurry. In the French manner, signs to Paris appeared in the most out of the way places.

There were just the two of them. The lorry he was following and himself. A flash of red braking lights and a cloud of smoke from the tyres slowed the lorry. The driver signalled to go left but swung to the right blocking the road.

Glad I didn't choose that moment to over take, Hedley thought.

The driver got out of his cab, checking his distance from the gateposts and gave Hedley a cold stare of annoyance, before climbing back into his cab.

The revving diesel engine shattered the peace of the forest and black smoke polluted the air. With a sudden jolt, the lorry shuddered back onto the drive beside the house and was gone. The smell of burning diesel was all that remained.

Hedley looked at the map, which pointed to the coast. In twenty minutes there was the sea but not just the sea, Atlantic breakers crashed onto the golden sand set against the high dunes. Here was the best surfing centre this coast had to offer. Glamour and wealth on show with the beautiful people sunbathing, swimming, and strutting curvaceously along its pretty shoreline.

Hedley felt a curious mixture of desires but one of the most urgent now was to eat and drink. Le Touring Café offered everything he needed. At a suggestion to take a seat in the corner overlooking the street and the sea, he needed no second bidding. The menu of entrees and Specialites Fruit de Mer filled him with high expectations. This was a mini gastronomic heaven.

Hedley settled down taking in the surroundings. As he sipped the beer he had ordered, a waft of smoke rose from the terrace below. He hadn't smoked in twenty years yet at that moment there was a sudden urge to fill his lungs with that seductive pleasure. He looked down. The smoker a girl, pretty dress, feminine, sophisticated, had an air about her that suggested an energetic drive. Perhaps a follower of some cause or revolutionary leader?

She looked up and Hedley smiled but it was not returned, in fact the total opposite. The, 'keep away if you know what's good for you look!' Hedley shrugged his shoulders and turned away but couldn't resist a sideways glance. A scraping of chairs on the floor, the jolt of the table and a, "Hello," in a low whisper made the girl half stand and kiss her companion. He was a suave man who would grace the high table of any politician. The conversation rose in intensity not aggressive but passionate. The couple became aware that they were attracting attention and leaned more closely together. Their conversation took on a more conspiratorial air. Out of a holdall the man produced some photos and notes. Hedley's curiosity was raised by these events. Then a man walked along the street with a newspaper and mac over his arm. Strange Hedley thought, it's a bit hot for a mac and there's no sign of rain.

Two pops not quite the sound of a car backfiring but loud enough to make people curious. These were followed by a groan as the couple on the terrace below seemed to slump together in a curious embrace. Ah! two lovers getting carried away. The illusion of calm was soon shattered by loud screams. Blood was pouring from the couple's bodies. Sirens could be heard distant at first, but rapidly increasing in volume.
The waiter was offering what assistance he could, but it was obvious to Hedley that they were dead.
The police seemed to appear from nowhere.

"Did anyone see anything?" they shouted.

"No nothing." said the waiters. "It all happened so quickly."

"Perhaps a revenge killing?" suggested one customer at the next table.

"And you monsieur, your papers please. Did you see anything?"

Yes he thought but I am not saying anything, as he looked at the black beret on the floor next to the couple who had been shot.

He did have some information that would have been very useful but it would have exposed him. He wasn't supposed to be in Hossegor but neither was the man who had slipped out the back before the police arrived. He needed to get back to his lorry in the midst of the forest.

Hedley went over to the phone and dialled a London number then after a brief conversation, dialled another one...mine.

"Get on the next plane to Biarritz. I will meet you. I have a parcel for you to get back to London."

"Who was that on the phone darling?"

"It had better not be Hedley and no, you are not going to disappear on a wild goose chase."

I let out a quiet sigh of exasperation...how was I going to square the circle on this one with the two people I most cared for in this world?

BIOGRAPHY

Michael Palmer

In 1934 my father's boss told him that he was his best painter and decorator, but there was no work.
A year later father was an Aircraftsman in the R.A.F. and posted to R.A.F. Tangmere.
Our family grew with one brother and a sister, moving every 18 months to another R.A.F. station.
My earliest relocation was on a very cold night. 24 December 1949 (the date is accurate as it was stamped in my mother's passport).
We were off to RAF Gatow on the boundary between the Russian and the British sector. Berlin was a city of vast contrasts. Supreme opulence courtesy of the Americans, contrasted with derelict buildings and deprivation for its citizens...
Everything was on offer for 200 fags, my Dad's weekly ration.

It was a great shock back in Chettle, a rural village, when I asked for a Mars bar in the shop.
"Where's your ration book sonny?" I began to learn a stark lesson of the 'have and have nots.' A lesson I have never forgotten.

I enjoy short stories, not much good with poetry and get bored at the idea of a full blown novel.
Hope you enjoy the book that we have worked hard to produce.

mike@microbite.co.uk

INTRODUCTION

GLENYS MASON

1. The Last Walk
Demonstrating the importance of describing the use of the senses: Touch, Smell, Sight and Feelings conveying this to the reader.

2. The Groaning Nest
Having picked this title in a random lucky dip; I have written a children's story around it.

3. Contrary Mary
This is a twist on a well known children's story.

4. Rosie Rabbit
A children's story.

5. Biography

THE LAST WALK

The smell of Johnson's baby soap sticks in my nostrils, and I savour every moment while bathing you carefully. I watch you as you contentedly suck at my breast. You watch me with those big brown eyes and I bend to nuzzle my face into your soft, dark curly hair.I sniff the lovely baby smell of you, and a sob catches in my throat because it's time, the hour I have been dreading.

Such a good baby; you never cry unless you are hungry. A small whimper leaves your lips as if you sense something is wrong.

Six weeks we have had together, locked in our own little world in this awful cold home run by nuns who never say a kind word to us. How can they say they are doing God's work? They tell me what a wicked girl I am, and that you will be better off without me.

I keep thinking of the moment I first held you, it was love at first sight, so perfect in every way, those tiny shell-like ears, the rosebud mouth that curls in a lopsided grin when you have wind, at least I'm told that's what you have.

Little fingers that grip around mine, I feel my heart tighten, and my throat feels sore with unshed tears, how can I let you go? But I am sixteen years old with no prospects, and no money of my own.

Mum says that Dad agreed I could go home but that

I could not take you with me. I have to give you up for adoption.

Dressing you in a white romper suit and the white matinee jacket that I knitted for you, it looks as if you are ready for your christening, and in a way you are; who knows what your new parents will name you.

To me you will always be my Mark; that's because you have made an indelible mark on my life one which can never be erased.

Now we must take our last walk together along the path to the end of the garden into the lodge house. Once we go through that door you will be taken from me and handed over to someone else, a new beginning and I hope a happy life.

For me it will be like the end of my world, I cannot imagine life without you. The tears fall, loud sobs come from my throat, it feels like I'm on the periphery looking on at this horrific scene.

The door slams shut in my face, my gorgeous little boy torn from me forever.

THE GROANING NEST

Mother Blackbird flew into the tiny nest, landing heavily as her chicks squawked loudly. Stretching out their necks, wanting to be fed on the fat worm wiggling in her beak.

Watching the chicks eating, she could not help noticing that one of her brood was very big. It was almost three times the size of the other two, and she was sure she had laid more than three eggs. The huge chick looked nothing like the others!

The nest was groaning under the weight of them all. Mother Blackbird flew back and forth with moss and twigs, trying to repair the nest and make it stronger. She also worked hard finding food to feed the chicks, but there never seemed to be enough to go around.

One day Mother Blackbird arrived at the nest with a big juicy grasshopper in her beak; On the nest she saw the large chick push one of the small ones' head first out of the nest.

Dropping the food, she cried, "You can't do that." The large chick snatched the grasshopper up in its mouth before flying away from the nest.

It was a baby cuckoo. The mother Cuckoo never builds a nest of her own; instead, she lays one large egg in another bird's nest.

The bird that has built the nest does not notice the

difference between the bigger egg and her own. She feeds and looks after all the babies until they are strong enough to fly away, The cuckoo chick pushes the other babies out of the nest when it gets the chance, to make sure it has extra food.

Mother Blackbird, looking worried, went to check her last remaining, tiny little chick and wondered if it would be strong enough to survive.

Rushing to and fro with little grubs and flies, she fed the tiny chick until he was strong and had grown feathers so that he could fly from the nest whenever he wanted. One day that's exactly what he did.

The nest, now empty, no longer groaned, and Mother Blackbird snuggled down in it for a well-earned rest.

CONTRARY MARY

Mary is such a contrary old lady, she is so pedantic about everything, and over the years she has driven her family, friends and neighbours away. Nothing ever pleases her, she finds fault with just about everything and everyone.

Home is a little cottage in the pretty seaside village of Polperro in Cornwall.

The one thing that does bring happiness to Mary is her garden. Every day come rain or shine she toils outside tending it.

She is very neat and tidy never a thing out of place, the flowers grow in straight lines, and seashells lay between the rows strategically placed to separate each type of plant.

Silver bells on rods placed in the earth jingle gently in the breeze to scare off the birds, mostly seagulls, from pecking at her precious plants.

Mary is happy in her solitude; as long as she has her garden nothing else seems to matter.

Then one evening whilst watering her plants, she tripped over a conch shell half hidden in the soil.

She fell landing heavily on her left leg; suffering excruciating pain she could not move. Fearing she had probably broken her hip, she looked around frantically calling out to anyone that may be passing.

The neighbours had gone away, and anyway she had upset everyone she came in contact with, so nobody would miss not seeing her around.

Hours passed slowly, Mary was in pain, hungry, and tired, she began to weep. It was her own fault she had no friends, feeling sorry for herself she realised that if she survived the night, things would definately have to change.

By now it was the early hours of the morning and Mary was almost unconscious. The milkman arrived at the back door to deliver her usual pint of milk. As it was Friday he knocked for his weekly payment.
Receiving no answer he turned to walk away, but then noticed the heap laying on the ground amongst the immaculate flowerbeds.

Rushing over he knelt beside Mary, and shouted to passers-by for help. Soon an ambulance arrived and amidst much yelling, Mary was taken to hospital. “What about my garden, my flowers? Nobody will care for them as much as I do?”

“Don’t you worry Mary, the neighbours will rally, and we will see that everything is taken care of.”
During the weeks that followed, the villagers wrote out a roster and all took turns at visiting the hospital and doing the gardening duties.

Mary had time to reflect on her attitude towards people and made a promise to herself that from now on, she would mend her ways.

Once back home she joined the Agricultural Society and offered help to those starting out in their gardens or allotments. It gave her a new sense of achievement when she heard those words;

“Mary Mary how does your garden grow?”

ROSIE RABBIT

Becky had been ill for a long time; she had something called Leukaemia and every few weeks she had to go into hospital to have some special medicine, which was put into her body through her arm.

Often, she was frightened and cried at these times, and she would squeeze her favourite toy Rosie Rabbit, tight to her chest. A little paw would rest in Becky's neck and Rosie would whisper in her ear, "Everything will be alright."

Becky's Daddy had bought Rosie Rabbit as a present for her when she was a tiny baby. She had loved the fat, fluffy, snuggly rabbit for as long as she could remember, Mummy said, even as a little baby she held Rosie tightly in her arms when she went to sleep, and when she started walking she dragged Rosie everywhere she went. One thing Becky would never do was go to sleep without her dearest little rabbit.

One night when Becky had finished her medicine, she was sick all over the bed, her clothes and all over Rosie. The nurses came and gently changed Becky's nightdress and put clean sheets on the bed. In all the commotion nobody seemed to notice that Rosie was disappearing into the bag of dirty washing.

Where was Rosie going? The bag was pushed into a sort of dark cupboard and suddenly she was whizzing down a noisy slide, only not like the one in the park!

She landed with a bump in a hot, steamy noisy room. She tried to wriggle out from under the heap of washing.

Oh No! Now what was happening? Hands were pushing her into a machine, poor Rosie clung to the sides of the door as she was whisked round and round in the hot soapy water, her eyes rolling, she felt quite dizzy.

Having been through first hot, then cold water, whooshed and spun round and round, Rosie lay exhausted among the tangle of clean laundry.

Big hands pulled and separated the washing and Rosie fell with a bump onto the floor. "What have we here?" said the laundry man. A cute fluffy rabbit, it must have been put in the laundry bag by mistake. Perhaps it belongs to someone on the children's ward? I'll phone and ask if anyone has lost a toy rabbit."

Poor Becky had cried all night. She could not, would not sleep, without her precious Rosie. Everyone looked around the ward, mummy had tried looking under the bed, in the cupboards, even in her handbag, but Rosie was nowhere to be seen.

Then one of the nurses had remembered changing the bedclothes the day before and that gave them a clue as to what had happened. The phone rang, and a nurse came to tell them that Rosie had been found.

Everyone was so pleased that Rosie Rabbit had been returned to Becky, who hugged her tightly and promised Rosie she would never let her out of sight again.

Rosie was so happy to be back with Becky after her adventure in the hospital laundry. The only good thing about it was that Rosie was clean, fluffy and looking rather pretty!

BIOGRAPHY

Glenys Mason

Originally from Kent, and after years as an army wife abroad, I finally put down roots in Essex.

Having worked as a qualified nurse for many years, I took a degree as an Occupational Health Nurse Practitioner and followed this occupation until I retired. I now help as a volunteer for the local Alzheimer's Group.

I became a member of the Ongar Writing Circle a few years ago. I wanted to write children's stories for my granddaughter. Being part of the writing circle has helped me to improve my technique.

They say there is a novel in all of us; this is my starting point, feeling my feet, working towards the Big One.

glenysmason@uwclub.net

INTRODUCTION

MICHAEL SHEARER

1. The Old Man

2. She Who Was Once The Helmet-Maker's Beautiful Wife

3. The Stones Of Santiago

4. The Ten Virtues Of Porridge

5. Openings

7. Biography

THE OLD MAN

My father (he was never Dad) could be funny, even witty sometimes.

When I was about five or six, we lived in a slum in North London. It was over a garage. You went around the back, down a rubbish-strewn alley, then first right into the yard. Hefty coal bins to the left, massive fire-escape (because of the garage) to the right up to our kitchen window on the third floor. My regular entrance.

Straight ahead, the front door for all the families. A dark hall with post boxes & electric meters. Then a curving staircase to the doors on the first floor, another staircase to the second, a shorter one to our own door.

One Sunday, my father and I were sitting in the living room when the door bell rang. Way down below. Unusual.I scurried after him on my little legs.
At the door was a scruffy young man in a flat hat.

“Merry Christmas, Sir,” said the man, touching his cap, “I’m the man who empties your dustbin.”

“Merry Christmas,” replied my father, “I’m the man who fills it up.”

He shut the door, firmly.

We got rubbish strewn around the yard for weeks.

More common was a mood so foul that you couldn't talk to him at all, about anything. These filthy moods would last for days. Mother got the worst of it. I just kept out of his way. You could go out to play all day then, in any weather.

He did go to the doctor about it once. He was examined & the doctor mused: "Tell me, Mr. Leary, do you drink at all?"

"Well, I like a pint."

"How many, typically?"

"Oh, maybe a dozen."

"Hm, that's not so bad. Twelve pints a week."

"No, no, a night."

"I see."

He cut back briefly, but the old habits returned. There was something else going on, something strong.

He never missed a day's work. A glazier. Up ladders carrying massive sheets of glass, on to roofs. Hard physical labour. You can work off the effects of the night before like that. He had huge, powerful hands, thickly callused, like built-in gloves.

He tried to teach me how to be manly.

"Men have to look after girls & women," he told me earnestly, "We must take care of them, protect them, keep them safe. That's being a Man."

I believed him.

Then he would go out, have his twelve pints, come home and beat up my mother.

I could hear it, lying in bed, in the attic above.

"Oh, don't, John. Please John, don't. Please don't." A horrible pleading. Then the terrible thumps, & the sobs.

The shame was overwhelming. It was my duty to go down there. To protect her, stand up to him, despite his wide shoulders & massive hands. Put my little body between them. Challenge him. I didn't have the courage. I cried myself to sleep in pity for my mother & with the conviction that I was a coward. Not a Man at all.

I took all this as normality.

Kids were like that in those days.

He beat me too. His belt usually. For what seemed to me to be such trivial things that they weren't really wrong at all. Dropping a fork on the floor at the dinner table maybe.

I decided that my only way of getting back was to show no response. I didn't cry, didn't whimper, didn't call out; not even a grunt, not the slightest noise. Dry eyed & defiant. He gradually packed it in.

She tried to leave him. I remember once being dressed up in my Sunday best on a weekday. Stiff, black shoes, heavy overcoat. She packed a small suitcase & out we went on a bitterly cold winter's afternoon; ice & snow. We walked the streets, up and down & round & about. I had no idea what was going on. Was trained not to ask. We finally came to a stop outside the Electric Company opposite the Public Baths. The trouble was, she didn't really have anywhere to go. Only to her sister or her mother, both of whom would have sent her back to her husband.

Women were like that in those days.

We walked back, slowly.

He applied for a council house when I was born. We moved into a maisonette when I was thirteen. Our first bathroom. We thought it was luxury.
I was becoming adolescent, more challenging. We had blistering arguments, about anything at all. Whether submarines would work in fresh water as well as the sea, for example. I would work him round

to contradict himself, then he'd deny he'd ever said what had started the 'discussion'.

Once I wrote out what he claimed & got him to sign the statement. An hour later, he was saying the opposite. I retrieved the signed slip of paper & held it up to him with a smug grin on my face. There was an animal roar & he was up and coming for me. I fled, fast, out the room, up the stairs with him a couple of steps behind. Into the bathroom, door slammed & locked. He came straight through the locked door as if it wasn't there.

"Stop. Stop, you'll kill me!"

He froze with one massive fist already on its way. His face twisted & twitched in conflict until he backed off, went downstairs & down the pub.

I tried to leave him also. When it came to university I went to York. Two hundred miles north. Hoping it was enough.

When I eventually returned, I slowly, incrementally, became his drinking partner. His old pals were dying off, moving away.

Towards the end of the night usually, things got said, leaked through his defences. It took years to get the big picture. He'd had a bad war, a tough war. He'd seen a lot of his mates killed, blown up, mutilated.

Flame-throwers were the worst, he said. He'd killed a lot of people himself. Not all of them were German, not all of them were male, not all of them were adult.

He had indignantly refused to take his medals.

"Bits of tin for men's lives," he would say, bitterly.

Not like that in the beginning. He had volunteered, though underage, like every other young man in his street.

Men did that sort of thing in those days.

There followed vigorous basic training, designed to destroy the individual will so that you obeyed orders, even if it meant certain death.

Then off to North Africa. The greatest blood-bath, he said was the Battle of Long Stop Hill. Then enshipped to Sicily for six weeks of moderate killing; leading to the landings in Italy.

Inland & north, fighting all the way, pushing the Germans back, the length of Italy. Monte Casino was the most brutal, but it was all bad.

People forget the sheer physical hardship. Not sleeping for days sometimes, no washing to speak of, same clothes indefinitely. Rations on the good days; living off the land mostly.

One evening, a patrol he was in came across a pig. They held it down, squealing like rending metal, & hacked off its leg, leaving it to bleed to death. Took the joint back to cook for all.

Once, high in the wintry Italian mountains, he awoke blind. His eye-lids had frozen shut. A friend peed on his eyes so he could ease them open.

They would attack a village, the Germans would fight for a while & then retreat to the next. Sometimes they left behind a suicidal unit to delay the Allied advance. You never knew. There might be snipers, booby traps.

I recall late one night sitting with him in one of the Victorian pubs of London. Round tables with wrought iron legs, dark wood shelving behind the bar, the pub's name in bevelled lettering in glass, scintillating light from chandeliers.

He sat slightly hunched, still wearing his overcoat. His heavy hands before him on the table, palms up, curved like a couple of begging bowls. He stared down into them, but not seeing them, seeing what those hands had done in a hot, half-demolished village in Italy.

"You walk with all your senses on alert, like an animal. Death can come from anywhere. I picked my way over some rubble into the main street. There were farm carts all smashed, bits of glass, rags, bodies, bits of bodies. The stink of death. Then something clicked to my left. I turned & fired, one movement. It was instinctive."

He sighed & his rheumy eyes moistened. His voice got throaty and gruff.

"It wasn't a German soldier," he breathed, "it was a little girl."

"Instinct," he pleaded, "just instinct."

SHE WHO WAS ONCE THE HELMET-MAKER'S BEAUTIFUL WIFE

She married young, very young.

It was inevitable.
She attracted men like bees to lavender;
they became intoxicated,
their male armour fell from them;
they flitted around her, skinless,
with tender cretinous grins,
and minds
disabled by erotic innocence.

She knew not what she did.

In those days
he who was to be
the helmet-maker
made gates and railings,
pounding metal, arms
like girders.

Only after the wedding
did he suffer from the sight
of the wounds of warriors,
wince at sunsets,
stand captured and helpless,
open-mouthed in pain,
before scrawny fledglings,
or the gentle green
of new growth.

His work became more delicate
and ornamented with scrolls
and tendrils, exotic beasts
and many an occult sign,
which he intuitively hoped
might fend things off.

Weapons at first,
blades to die for,
then shields
with decoration which tried to talk magic
with the world.

And finally,
the exquisite works
which made his fame
and caused his death.

She went a little crazy,
would kiss flowers
and talk to streams;
became thin as a shard,
then fat as a barrel,
grew pomegranates,
and never spoke again.

THE STONES OF SANTIAGO

There are stones on the way to Santiago.
There are stones all the way to Santiago.
But the stones are not pebbles,
The stones are not boulders,
The stones are not mountains.

The stones are a hardness of the heart
And are carried in the soul.

Every chance to take that's taken.
Every chance to give forsaken.
These are your stones, pilgrim,
These are your very own stones.

THE 10 VIRTUES OF PORRIDGE

It lacks vanity.
It tells no lies.
It stays in the bowl.
It sits thoughtless.
It bears no grudges.
It takes no vengeance.
It is faithful to its kin.
It has no debts.
It drinks only milk.
It serves another.

OPENINGS

Once, in Portugal,
walking through thick forest;
tall trees and many branches
covering the sky,
save for one patch of blue,
which found its kin
deep within
and each knew
and was not alone.

Once, in Hackney,
emerging from a rough pub
into the snow-filled streets,
seeing a single red rose
spot-lit by a lamp-post;
and the rose knew its echo
far forward in time
and knew its rhyme
in the world's poem.

Once in Galicia,
raising my eyes
from a field of maize
seeing small, dark figures
toiling in the landscape
making notes on a stave
whose music was played
in all our days.

Once in Florence
when a painted angel's gaze
shook down my walls
and I was naked
and not ashamed
and knew I'd always been home
and had never left it.

And all these times
are the same time
in the place that is once only
always.

BIOGRAPHY

Michael Shearer

Born just post-war and brought up in a slum in East London. School which also included Eric Bristow, Michael Caine, Harold Pinter. Degree in Philosophy and Literature (York). Many jobs - builder's labourer, factory operative (filing cabinets, briefcases, ladies' hats), clerk, security guard. College lecturer in Logic, Philosophy, English. Hobby: Long-distance walking. Retired. I read (10,000 books indoors), think, go down the pub, write, grow vegetables. Many publications. 'Walking a Rainbow' on YouTube. Married 50 years. No TV. No mobile. Lots of time!

mshearer@postmaster.co.uk

INTRODUCTION

HEATHER LEWIS

1. Celebrating Essex

2. Halcyon Days

3. I Wish I Could Have Asked You, Gran

4. Broken Dreams

5. Souvenir

6. Gratitude

7. Biography

CELEBRATING ESSEX

I'm celebrating Essex, the county I call home,
I've lived within its borders since the day that I was born.
I've been abroad for holidays, and travelled in UK
But home's always been Essex, and for me that's quite OK.

A childhood spent in Toppesfield, a quiet village place
With farmers' fields, a central pump, and lanes down which to race.
Thatched cottages and wonky roofs, and primrose woods around
A lovely place to grow up, so very safe and sound.

Holidays with cousins, in Westcliff, near the sea,
Fun on the beach was had by all, but a long walk back for tea!
Sometimes we travelled northward, to Durham and Wallsend,
But Essex always called us, and our homeward way we'd wend.

I had to leave my village home to go and work away,
For there were no jobs in childcare that I could reach each day
So off I went to Woodford Bridge, and a residential home,
To care for little children with no families of their own.

While there I went to college, and life was very sweet,
And I met the man who very quickly swept me off my feet.
We set up home in Harlow, so I stayed an Essex girl,
With a husband, home, and children, and life was such a whirl.

We're both retired now, and still live in Harlow town
Near our children and grandchildren, most of them fully grown.
I look out of my window and a busy road I see
And beyond it is the common, lots of trees
and greenery.

We often roam the county's roads, to see what we can see,
In sunshine and in rain, Essex is a great place to be.
It's home to us, we love it, all the roads with ups and downs,
That lead us to those villages, and lovely country towns.

So I'm celebrating Essex, the place that I call home,
The county that I've lived in, and on its roads have roamed.
And when life on earth is over, I'll lie beneath the grass,
In the Harlow cemetery, so I'll stay an Essex lass!

HALCYON DAYS

Ah halcyon days,
On the fringes of my memory
Shrouded in the mists
Of time gone by
Those days of sunlight on the sea
Water lapping on the boat's side
You and I
Lounging on the deck
With wine and food laid out before us
Nothing to do
But relax
And enjoy the leisured time.

We could lay late in bed
Snuggled in the cosy cabin
With a cup of coffee
Watching through the window
As the boats sailed out
To fish,
Or take the tourists round the bay
Such lovely days I still recall
Strolling in the town
Meeting friends
Sitting outside the café on the harbour wall.

Where did those days go?
How have they passed so quickly
From reality
Into a distant memory?
What changed our world so much
That now our home is not a boat
But a terraced house
In a suburban street

The answer lies upstairs
He's sleeping now
But soon he'll wake
And cry for us
To bring him down to play.

For we have a son,
And so we've had to come back
To the normal humdrum world.

But would we go back to those halcyon days?
Not now, it's just not possible
When we have a child
And another soon will join our family.

If we still lived on the boat
There would be problems.

No schools along the harbour side
No playgrounds
With swings and slides
And no place to keep the children's toys.
Our boat is stored,
Laid up and unused now.

But maybe later
When our family has grown
And flown the nest
We will return to lazy days in the sun.

I WISH I COULD HAVE ASKED YOU, GRAN

I wish I could have asked you, Gran,
I've got so many questions all about your life.
My memory of you is a calm and gentle soul,
But my family history research
Shows your early life was hard.

Born to parents who, it seems, had money,
But you were the only child,
And then they separated
When you were young and still at school.

Your life must have changed so much!
Scrubbing doorsteps in the morning before school
So that your mother could buy gin.
What drove her to that, I wonder?

Where was your home, Gran?
No Census for those years.
But then I found your mother in a Rescue Home,
Trying to give up the 'demon drink'
And you were with your father's father,
How did that come about?

How and where did you meet my Grandpa?
Did you wait long to marry?
For you were 27 on your wedding day,
and he was 24.
Did you hope life would be easier for you,
with a husband at your side?

I Wish I Could Have Asked You, Gran

I wonder how you felt about the constant moving that you had to do
I know it was because of Grandpa's job,
but hard for you,
Settling in one place for a year or two,
Then moving on again, with little children now in tow.

1914, and the call to arms
Did you stand by him when he went to war,
And left you with the children, four by then,
Did you argue and plead, or send him off
with a smile,
While worrying and wondering if he would return?

I wish I could have asked you, Gran,
What it was like when he came back.
Your daughters told me he was changed,
So nervous and short-tempered,
Never speaking of his experiences at the Front.

I wonder often if this was the reason
That you settled in one place,
So that Grandpa could start his own tailor's shop
Instead of working for others.
In 1925 you moved from London out to Harlow,
With five children, your mother, and a sixth child due
in just a month!
How did you manage that, Gran?

Were the next years as quiet as you'd hoped?
Your children growing up and moving on,
making their own lives.
Another war to live through,
Three of your six children actively involved,
More worries for you, Gran.

I wish I could have asked you, Gran,
What kept you strong through all the trials
of your life?
I was only seven when you died,
But I recall the sweet and gentle lady that you were.
I've pieced together all that I can find,
And one day
I'll write your life in tribute to you, Gran.

BROKEN DREAMS

We sat in the half-dark room,
Lit only by the moonlight shining through the skylight above us.
Always afraid now of what might happen.
We talked softly of our hopes and dreams,
Yet knowing that we might never achieve them.

Alyssa was studying medicine, longing to be a doctor,
To help others,
I dreamed of being a dancer in the ballet
And I loved my lessons and my practice.
Benjamin wanted to teach,
To share with children his own love of history.
Mama and Papa smiled on us,
Encouraging our talk, taking our minds briefly away
From the terror that might come at any time.

This garret was our home, had been now for months.
The friends who helped us brought food, took away our rubbish, and generally cared for us in secret.

The terror came, as we always, deep in our minds, knew it would.
It arrived late one night,
Darkness, always the time of evil doings, and of fear.
Loud footsteps on the stairs -
Heavy boots crashed against the door
Sending my father flying across the room.
He'd tried to bar the way,
But no-one could withstand their onslaught.
We were roughly seized, dragged out into the street.

A wall of sound assailed our ears -
Shouts and jeers from those who once had been our friends, our neighbours,
They watched from underneath the street lamp
As we were thrown into the lorry
Falling, screaming, fearful.

Others were already in there,
My friend Marya, and her brother Josef,
Their parents too, and the old woman from the flat below.
Poor Mrs. Walesa, what had she ever done to harm anyone?
Where had she been hiding?
Had friends helped her, as they had us?
And what would happen to those friends
If it was discovered they had helped us?

But this was the horror that we'd feared,
We didn't fit their 'ideal race' so we were just taking up time and resources
That could be used by their favoured ones.

We sat ourselves up in the lorry as much as we could,
Those already inside making room for us
And squeezing hands and arms in an attempt to comfort.
We braced ourselves against the tailboard,
Ready to try and jump out,
To run from this if it were ever possible.

Yet we knew that from where we were being taken
There would be no turning back,
And all our dreams were gone.

SOUVENIR

A German helmet
Green with age,
And rusted,
Dented, holed
Turned up by the plough
In fields at peace for over a hundred years
But still remembered
As the site of many battles.
The man who wore this helmet
On the battlefield
Would surely not have lived
To tell his tales of war.

Rolfe was called from home
Like many others
So hard to leave his family,
Praying he'd survive
And come back to his wife and children
That there would soon be peace for all.

Training in the barracks
For so short a time
Then off to war
A tented camp his home for now.

Marching into battle
Fearful, wondering
What would happen
Would he survive this conflict?

In trenches
Bullets flying
Canons crashing
Shells exploding
Shouted commands,
Friends dying.

Horses screaming in their pain.
A friendly bullet to the brain
The only answer.

Sleepless nights
Under the stars
Those same stars shone over his homeland.

And always watching,
Watching for the enemy to come.
Resting when he could.
Gas mask at the ready,
Gas that both sides used
To try and make the enemy give in.

Rolfe lay trembling
Wondering why?
Why men fought
And killed each other
Just to prove a point?
To show their country's strength?

No sense in this, he thought,
And laid aside his helmet
Sick of all the filth and pain around him
Ready to give up and die.
The last great crash of shellfire that he heard
Blew the trench around him into pieces
Leaving him buried to the hips in mud,
His legs numbed by the shock,
He didn't know if he still had them.

Comrades dragged him out,
Flung him, and others,
Onto a wagon
Drawn by plough horses
To the field hospital.

Rest at last,
Exhausted, crying,
But grateful just to be alive.

From there, home to Germany
Thankful that he could still see,
And walk, and talk,
And hug his family,
Farm his land again.

Souvenir

His helmet lay
where he had laid it
Holed and battered
By the shell that had almost taken his life
Buried in the mud of Flanders
Where it lay till found by the French farmer
One hundred years later
In a world at peace?

GRATITUDE

I stood among them,
On that quiet sunny day
Those long white lines
In military precision,
All men and nations mingled here
Rank and regiment no longer mattered,
All equal now in death.

I stood among them,
Read the stories that those headstones told
Of men who died in war,
Fathers, sons and brothers
From so many families
And countries.

I stood among them
And I looked to see if there was any sign of light
From those horrific days of darkness.
I found some hope
In records of heroism on the battlefields,
And in the unity of all those buried here,
No matter how they fought.

I stood among them
Grateful that none of mine lay in this ground
This foreign soil,
Far from homes and loved ones.
Yet the thought came
'They are all mine'
For they are part of me.

I stood among them,
Watching the living among the dead.
Children running, playing,
While their parents read the gravestones
And the stories that they told
And older people standing,
Quietly remembering.

And I thanked them.

France. Since I wrote this I have done some more family history research and discovered I have a great-uncle who died on the battlefield in France and has no known grave. Subsequent visits to such cemeteries have been even more poignant).

BIOGRAPHY

Heather Lewis

Since childhood I've always loved words and seeing how they fit together to make sentences. Expressing my thoughts in writing satisfies a creative urge in me, and I enjoy spending time writing short stories and poetry. I can be inspired by small happenings, or by just a word or two. I'm not convinced I'll ever write a novel though!

When I was a child, my mother often said that one day she'd come in and find me reading a dictionary, and when it actually happened it became a family joke.

Prior to joining the Ongar Writing Circle I was part of Harlow Writers' Workshop, and contributed to the book 'Launching Rockets' aimed mostly at children. I have also entered several local writing competitions, and have gained a third prize in Age UK Essex competition (Poetry Section) two years running. I also entered a piece for the "Essex Belongs to Us" book, which was accepted.

I hope you enjoy my contributions to this book!

billandheatherlewis@yahoo.co.uk

INTRODUCTION

JANET OLIVER

1. Living In Essex

2. Holiday Contrasts

3. Presents

4. Nathan

5. A Stitch In Time
This was written in response to a task of writing on a chosen proverb.

6. Biography

LIVING IN ESSEX

Growing up south of the river, I knew nothing about Essex until I met my husband when I was at college. When he took me home to meet his parents, Essex was a housing estate in Witham, and long queues at the Army and Navy roundabout before they built the bypass. None of it seemed as picturesque as my part of Surrey, all of it seemed rather flat and boring and I don't think it would have occurred to me to visit it for pleasure.

Gradually, after we were married, I began to visit some other parts of the county; I discovered there were lovely villages like Finchingfield and even a few areas of higher ground with views! Maldon became a favourite place to visit, especially when we had children. They loved the swimming hole where my husband had learnt to swim years before. Now of course that has gone and the area is much tidier and probably safer, but there was a lot of charm in the simplicity of a day out there with a picnic, taking chairs for the grandparents and enjoying the sunshine. Nowadays we usually head for the Tiptree tea room at Heybridge Basin; we have sailed there ourselves on our boat and stayed the night (the lock is only useable near high tide) and enjoyed barbeques in the evening as the sun gradually slips behind the masts. There is something quite relaxing about knowing you cannot go anywhere for twenty-four hours except a walk along the towpath.

In the last few years we have got to know Burnham on Crouch as we keep our boat there. The low-lying ground allows wide views across huge areas of land.

Its charm grows on you over time – the landscape changes so much as the tide comes in and the mud disappears beneath the water for another few hours. A heron stabs into the mud as it patrols the shoreline. We sit on deck on a warm evening and listen to the sounds of the boatyard and the flocks of birds sweeping over us. Admittedly the frequent roar of orange planes turning overhead as they swoop down towards Southend is less romantic!

I am a history lover, and so have enjoyed trips to Colchester and other places down the years. I love some of the old buildings one comes across on a trip across the county, especially those with pargeting showing country scenes. Giant barns as at Cressing Temple astound with their size, while little village streets are lined with thatched cottages and half-timbered properties. We have lived in an Essex village for twenty years now. We have got to know people here, taken part in local events and joined local societies.

Perhaps because of our Witham connection, our travels have often taken us up the A12 rather than down the A13. I'm sure I've missed some lovely spots in that part of the county - sometime we must visit them. One change has happened so gradually I've hardly noticed it. For years, as we crossed the Thames going south I felt I was heading home. Now I realise - I am home.

HOLIDAY CONTRASTS

Golden light on marble floors drifts across the terrace.
Tables with white linen; ice clinks in tall glasses,
A deferential waiter bows and hands a menu.
We sit, contented, gazing at the view.
Boats drift below us, white triangles gleaming
In the sun,
Vesuvius looms through the mist,
An ominous presence.
One day all this may change – but for now
Seems timeless.
People have always sat here, gazing at the view.

Grey skies and racing waves. The boat butts through
The troughs and peaks.
Suddenly, the engine stops. We gaze a moment
In surprise
Drifting with the tide. Tools are grabbed but
Nothing works.
We hoist the sails and go with the wind, retracing
Our course.
Days in Dover, waiting for repairs. Time to stroll,
To chat, relax,
Gazing at the Channel view.

Blue skies and no wind as we motor up the river,
Follow the green buoys till we see the masts.
A sharp left turn and into the marina,
Step on the pontoon and tie up fast.
The engine stops and quiet descends
As we gaze around us. Walk ashore and stare.

Here, at Bucklers Hard, great ships were built
Huge wooden monsters, now long gone.
Ice-cream in hand, we watch the swans drifting
People have always sat here, gazing at the view.

PRESENTS

Because it's my birthday
They're coming to tea,
I expect they will bring
A present for me.

I know what they'll say
For it happens each year,
This is for birthday
and Christmas, my dear.

You can choose if you open
Or leave it till then,
It's so close to Christmas
We can't buy again!

A wardrobe for Sindy?
Some paper dolls too,
I have a whole school full
But more would still do.

I want a new book -
Or perhaps two or three,
In fact the whole series
Would be good for me.

I like plastic horses
With riders and saddles
I've made them a stable
From old cardboard boxes.

I don't really mind
What present I get
But I know what my aunt
And my uncle will set

On the table before me
With looks of great pleasure
As if they are giving
The world's greatest treasure!

It won't be a wardrobe
Or books or a horse -
No, 'cause I hate them -
A jigsaw, of course!

NATHAN

Life in miniature, cradled in my arms,

Forgotten feelings well within me.

Dark hair, smooth skin, asleep – and dreaming?

What must it be like, torn from total security

Into an unknown place?

Perhaps it's just as well we can't remember.

Swaddled in blankets, knitted with such love,

Blues and pinks to suit whoever it might be.

Muttering to himself, he waves a hand,

Gripping my finger tightly.

A cry begins, wavers, then fades away.

We hold our breath.

Conversation pauses, then resumes

As all is quiet.

We take turns, smiling, talking to him

As if he understands.

One day he will. One day he'll run away from us,

Jumping in the air, moving far beyond our arms.

Carpe diem.

A STITCH IN TIME

The V & A was crowded as always but she managed to get a ticket to the exhibition. Crossing through the entrance hall and the shop she weaved between the statues and monuments towards her objective. Soon she was inside, surrounded by textiles whose survival after so many years was almost a miracle. Copes, vestments, all kinds of church garments and, very occasionally, a secular survivor like the Black Prince's cloak. Finally she found herself in front of a screen. She stood and gazed at the display as it showed the piece of fabric hung in a glass case beside it. As she watched, the fabric, a heavily embroidered altar frontal, was pulled apart into several strips of different sizes. The image on screen transformed into a different shape, with gaps here and there but recognisable now as a garment. It was almost as if she was inside the screen…

Blanche was twenty-five when she first saw the baby princess, crying hopelessly. She rushed forward and began to rock the cradle, crooning a lullaby as she did so. The baby opened her eyes that had been screwed up tight and there was a pause. Then she smiled and Blanche smiled back. It was love at first sight. Blanche had come to court from her home on the Welsh borders with her aunt, Lady Troy, and remained at Elizabeth's side for the rest of her life. There were long, hopeless days in the Tower; waiting days at Hatfield Palace; happy days at the beginning of her reign and many, many confidential conversations as the years went by. Blanche was

Chief Gentlewoman of the Privy Chamber, a position of responsibility that involved more than just looking after the Queen's clothes, jewels and even her ferret! She was friendly with Sir William Cecil and was involved in protecting the Queen at all times.

Blanche grew up near the little church of St Faith's, Bacton, in Herefordshire, which was old when she attended, stone with a squat little tower. The village was typical of its time, with fields and farms, barns and cottages around it. A favourite walk was to the top of Newcourt Trump, an old motte and bailey castle, long abandoned but providing a vantage point from which to gaze at the gently rolling countryside. As she grew older, she began to think about one day returning there. At the age of seventy she made her will and commissioned a grand tomb in the Church, with herself kneeling beside the figure of a seated Elizabeth and an inscription,
'With maiden Queen a maid did end my life.'

And yet Blanche did not go home. Perhaps she'd been away too long? Her life had been at Court, not in rural Herefordshire, and so she stayed with Elizabeth, travelling with her or remaining in London, perhaps, if journeys became too difficult. She was 82 when she died and the Queen paid for her funeral and tomb in St Margaret's, Westminster. Perhaps she was unwilling to let her friend and confidante go far away from her, even now? However, Blanche's heart was returned to Bacton and at some point the

Queen sent a magnificent piece of cloth, worn in a famous portrait, as a gift to the Church.

...The strips of fabric turned and twisted and formed themselves into a magnificent skirt. The colours had faded but the beauty of the embroidery was still there for all to see. Her gaze returned to the original in its glass case. If only it were possible to go back and see it as it once was. But time had moved on and so must she - others were waiting for a closer look. She moved on to the next amazing piece.

BIOGRAPHY

Janet Oliver

I have always enjoyed writing, and joined the Ongar Writing Circle a few years ago. I had a piece accepted for the 'Essex Belongs to Us' volume in 2017, and also won the adult section of the Ongar News annual writing competition last year. I'm very happy to include a selection of pieces in this book. I belong to a drama group and have written and adapted plays for them. I teach English part time and this year I've been besotted by my new grandson.

ONGAR WRITING CIRCLE

Printed in Great Britain
by Amazon